Intrigue
in the
House
of Wong

[signature]

ISBN : 978-0-9815499-0-3

Cover and interior design by Christine Reynolds and Thomas Kwei. Printed in the U.S.A.

Intrigue
in the
House
of Wong

Amy S. Kwei

I am thankful for the help and inspiration I received in making this book:

First, my husband, for his technical and emotional support. Other angels are Marie Cantlon, Christine Reynolds, Judith Neuman, the Tuesday night Aspen Writers' group, the Tuesday Morning Writers, the Taconic Writing Group, Lisa Smith, Tamias Ben-Magid, Warwick Ford, and Dalia Geffen.

To Celia

If you can dream,
you can do it.
~Walt Disney

~*Chapter* 1~

BEFORE A SECOND bong could sound, the "Buddy Talk" window popped up. Wendy smiled and gulped down her favorite soft drink. She could hardly wait to see what Dee Sharp (otherwise known as Debbie) had to say.

Ever since her family had moved their restaurant, the House of Wong, from New York's Chinatown to the Upper East Side, Wendy would rush home after school every day. It took her just a few minutes to grab a snack from the kitchen, run to her room to unload her books, drop her flute case, and turn on the computer. Soon she was logged on and chatting away with her best friend.

Dee Sharp wrote: *God, Wendy. You're so lucky to be out of Chinatown! Kidnappers sent the Chin family a piece of blood-soaked flesh — it's supposed to be little Eddy's earlobe! He's only nine, so everyone's going crazy.*

Wendy (aka Kween Be) replied: *Ew, gross! Now what?*

Mrs. Chin just freaked out, Debbie informed. *She's been crying and going to all the neighbors asking for donations to raise ransom money.*

Did someone call the cops? Wendy asked.

No cops. So not cool to get involved with Immigration, Dee Sharp continued. *The Snake Heads brought the Chins into America illegally. These underworld beasts control everything here — rocking slime everywhere.*

Wendy remembered Eddy as a gruff, sullen boy with a flat face. He did not speak English and always played alone. She wondered if she should have spoken to him now and then. She wished she could teach these "fresh-off-the-boat" kids some English. But she never had any time. She had to help out in the family restaurant. Plus, she was afraid of being seen as too touchy-feely, so she hung back. Now she felt terrible. Eddy must be terrified — even if they hadn't cut off his earlobe. How could anyone treat a child like that?

Her heart pounded like a drum just thinking about it. Everyone knew the Chins had been schoolteachers in China. Now Mr. Chin was the cashier in the Golden Palace Restaurant, and Mrs. Chin pushed a dim sum cart there during lunch hours. If they were lucky, the Chins would pay back the Snake Heads in twenty years. Like so many other immigrants, they probably had trouble meeting the payments. And now their son had been kidnapped.

Kween Be chimed in: *Stinks! Are you dialed in? Can't we do anything?*

Dee Sharp answered: *Send money? Nothing myself, but will ask Mom.*

Okay. I'll send my Christmas money and speak to my parents.

<B.G.> Wendy gave Debby a Big Grin, keyboard style.

All right! You're native born and can do something. So how's life uptown?

Well, hello, just because we've moved doesn't mean we've left Chinatown. Everything's different here. We haven't even said "Hi" to any of our neighbors yet. Like Grandma says, we can only be sure of Our Own People.

Must be awesome to be living with the rich and famous, no?

Kween Be answered: *I wish. Like Grandma, Grandpa, and my parents even recognize any rich and famous people! They still watch the Chinese channels on TV. I'll tell you one thing for sure, people are really well dressed around here.*

Like in the magazines? Dee Sharp asked.

Yeah, rocking posh. Like, I looked in the window of this one store, and nothing had a price tag on it. Then hello, a shoe store had a big SALE sign in front — everything 50 to 80 percent off. So I walked in, and most shoes were still over $100!

Wow, no kidding! Yours truly bought her last pair of Nikes here on the street for 15 bucks!

Well, I wear my new Nikes to school and still feel shabby.

Awesome in a way. Good try, Number-One Girlfriend!

Wendy paused before typing. *Yeah, right, I always see people talking to each other on the street, only they look smarter.*

Not smarter. We're just as smart. But they just look — like, cool. Or as if they belonged, right?

Yeah, they belong all right. I wish I could do something so my family would feel they belong too.

Dee Sharp asked: *Your family's American, aren't they?*

For sure — fifth generation! Still, they think they're Chinese, like everyone in Chinatown.

That's because they've always lived here. I envy your new digs. Gotta practice piano. Mom's calling — wants to hear me banging away! Meet you in the chat room 9:30 tonight. Cheerio!

Bang away! The Flute Princess has to practice too. :).

Debbie and her family had emigrated from Hong Kong when that bustling metropolis was still a British colony. She carried an English passport and liked to mimic the English way of saying "Cheerio!" Some people thought she was snooty, but Wendy knew she was just being playful.

Wendy's friendship with Debbie had intensified after her family moved. While they had been classmates in Chinatown, there were always crowds of other kids around to interrupt or eavesdrop on their conversation. Someone's cousin might know another someone who happened to know the Wongs and give all their secrets away. Then there would be an uproar in the House of Wong. (Not that anyone in the family would scold or lift a finger to punish Wendy or her brother, Winston.) Grandpa would just give another lecture on the family's struggle to survive in America. Grandma would wrinkle her brow and look sorrowful. Father would flash his bulging eyes, and Mother would hang open her mouth as if she could not believe one of her children would ever do such a thing! Everyone would shout warnings that the House of Wong must not be shamed in the community. The family pride depended on the children's model behavior and success in school.

In truth, Wendy never dreamed of doing anything shocking or scandalous. She wanted to bring distinction to the family as much as her elders did, but always having to be the "sweet little girl" who pulled off all As in class could get boring. That's why she owned an on-line handle. Calling herself Kween Be meant she ruled a kingdom where she could "Be" anything she imagined.

Wendy returned to the kitchen for a snack. The family was gathered around the rosewood dining table, the sing-song lilt of their Cantonese dialect bouncing off the high ceiling and the bare white walls still waiting to be decorated.

"Cocaine is a serious matter!" Her father banged his fist on the round table.

"This is happening outside our restaurant. Why should we get involved?" Grandma waved her hand to dismiss the subject. "As I was saying, I went home — I mean Chinatown — this morning." Grandma visited her old neighbors every day, running errands and shopping for the family's groceries. "I gave Mrs. Chin fifty dollars to ransom her son. What a shame — vicious gangs preying on our own people! Do you think we could spare another hundred?"

"No, Ma," Wendy's father growled. "We cannot spare another penny because we have no income now. We need every dollar to renovate our restaurant. It is important that we open as soon as possible."

Wendy's mother glared. "Ma, you've already told us about the Chins' terrible situation. And you gave them money. Since no one has called the police, how can anyone really be sure the ear is Eddy's?"

Grandpa frowned. "This is our home now, and we have to concentrate on our own problems!"

Wendy's father continued. "There are people in the alleyway doing bad things — maybe smoking pot or even dealing drugs outside our restaurant. They'll bring us the wrong kind of publicity." He banged the table again.

"Whatever they're up to in our alley, they could bring down our whole neighborhood," Grandpa added. "Any hint that we somehow encourage drug traffic will certainly be bad for business!"

"Geez, I just saw two men lurking in the alley on my way home," Wendy joined in. "Were they dealing dope?"

Everyone greeted her voice with surprise. They had not noticed her entrance.

"They probably were," her father replied. "Mr. Lee told me to watch out for drug addicts on our street and in the alley next to our restaurant."

"I have an idea!" Wendy's mother widened her long eyes, motioning Wendy to sit down. "Remember when we first moved here, Wendy told us her bedroom was right next to the alley and she overheard one of our Chinese waiters, a *fokay*, selling liquor stolen from our restaurant?"

"Yeah, that was almost three weeks ago." Wendy recalled. "The acoustics in my room are great. I hear almost every breath taken down there."

Her mother turned to look at her. "In that case, you must let us know when you hear anything again."

"Agreed." Wendy loved to help. Her long eyes echoed her mother's, curling upward as if they were wings, and her lashes flapping up and down as she talked. "Although I think it would be better to catch them in the act and turn them in!"

"These people are dangerous," Grandpa whispered.

"Wendy, is there a way for you to signal us so we can know right away?" Her father's eyes brightened.

"I see what you mean. Perhaps something less dangerous. Let me think." Wendy wrinkled her button nose. "I can run in to tell you when I hear anything. But if I'm practicing, it would seem suspicious if I suddenly stopped playing. The crooks down there might get alarmed."

"You could play us a special tune — like a signal!" Her mother winked.

"All right, our special, secret code!" Wendy's voice rose with excitement. "I can play — let's say, the national anthem on my flute. Then you can call the police right away!"

"No, no. We'd better not get involved directly." Her father raked his fingers through his graying hair. "As soon as we hear, we'll alert Mr. Lee, and he can call the police and say he saw something suspicious while passing our street."

Both grandparents nodded in agreement. They had learned to be cautious and clever so as not to offend anyone. Often, mutual assistance, and sometimes intricate plans, were devised among trusted friends. This was done to ensure survival in a land they felt treated them like foreigners.

Mr. Lee was a *ton heung* — a compatriot from the same village. He was an old bachelor with no family of his own. Everyone considered him part of the House of Wong. Born in Shamchun Village, he had learned shoemaking in Hong

Kong. When he first came to America, he was already a rich man, unlike the other new immigrants. Once in New York, he decided manufacturing ordinary shoes in the city would not be profitable. Instead, he offered personal service designing fancy boots in an upper-class neighborhood. He insisted on naming his store Lee Kee Boots because the name had brought him good fortune in Hong Kong.

"Leaky boots!" Wendy howled when she first heard the name. "He'll be out of business in a month!!!"

"Don't be fresh!" Her mother had looked at her fiercely. "Mr. Lee is a successful businessman. If a name brings him good luck, then he must stick to it."

Strangely enough, Lee Kee Boots became famous around town. Many wealthy people and show business personalities bought Mr. Lee's "leaky" boots, handcrafted from leather, silk, sable, mink, and even exotic materials like ostrich feathers.

"I told you," said her mother, wagging a triumphant finger at Wendy. "Mr. Lee has a good head for business. We have much to learn from him."

When they moved uptown, above East Ninety-sixth Street, Mr. Lee began coming to dinner almost every evening.

"I'm sure Mr. Lee will help us with our difficulties," her father said.

Wendy rose from her seat. Grandma brought in a plate of fried dough sticks and placed it in front of her.

Wendy was famished. She wrapped a dough stick in a napkin, munching on it as she walked back to her room. She couldn't wait to tell Debbie about their scheme to catch drug dealers, but a little voice inside warned her to wait. Tonight she would ask for more details about the kidnapping.

The girls preferred to talk through the Internet. The grown-ups approved when children used high-tech machines they didn't understand. They assumed the youngsters were doing home-work. Besides, Wendy wanted to talk to her close friend in private, without anyone looking over her shoulder or listening in.

All that talk about drug dealing and kidnapping had made Wendy uneasy. She opened the window that faced the solid brick wall of another building. There was no scenic view to distract her. The narrow alley below created a wind tunnel, which carried a good breeze. As she practiced her flute with the window open, the brick wall bounced the sound right back to her. She felt she might be playing in Carnegie Hall.

The kitchen downstairs opened onto the alley. Last week, when Mr. Wong held a meeting there with the other cooks to escape the construction noise, Wendy treated them to a free concert. Afterward, her father hollered "Bravo, bravo!" and the other cooks all gave her a round of applause. Wendy knew that when summer came, they would step out for air more often and would hear her music. Though too shy to admit it, she enjoyed having an audience.

Halfway down the first page in the overture from *Fiddler on the Roof*, she heard voices rising from the alley.

"You wan' some snow, don't you?"

"Yeah, tha's what I want . . ."

Did they mean cocaine? Wendy wondered. Her foot beat in time with the metronome, as she continued playing softly without missing a note.

"This' the best. Only jus' arrived," said the first voice.

"Sure, tha's what they all say," replied the second.

"Take a snort and see for y'self."

"Ah . . . that IS good!"

"This good, only two grand. It'd be three easy from the Duke."

Oh, no . . . should I play the "Star-Spangled Banner?" Wendy thought nervously. She was sure these characters were doing shady business down there. As her music wafted through the air, she thought it would sound too strange to switch from "Sunrise, Sunset" to "Oh, say can you see." Wendy finished the phrase and drew a deep breath.

"Yeah, good. Need a job; I got no dough," the second voice complained.

"Take out a loan. Boss says there's a job comin' up ta knock off some political creep — some foreign big shot."

"Tell your boss I wan' in. How much is he payin'?"

"Big dough. That's the talk."

Yes, here's a good place to switch tunes. Wendy began playing the national anthem. She was so agitated that she skipped several notes. *Keep on playing!* She urged herself. *I'm not really performing for anyone. Just play loud. Oh, but I sound like a total amateur! Do I have to play it all the way to the end? Yes, yes . . . give them time to call the police. But no, they're not calling the police, they're calling Mr. Lee. Mr. Lee must be calling the police now. Maybe I should take a quick look to see if anyone from the kitchen is out there. Dad should be informed . . .*

When she finished sounding the alarm, she laid down her flute, tiptoed to the window, and put her head out very slowly. The alley was empty.

"Did you call Mr. Lee? Did you call Mr. Lee?" Wendy ran into the kitchen, shouting and pulling her mother's sleeve. "Are the cops on their way?"

Wendy's parents were cooking dinner. They looked surprised. "Did you hear anything?" they asked each other.

"But I played the anthem!" Wendy's heart hammered between each word. She hopped and pointed toward her room. "I just heard the drug dealers!"

"The dishwasher and exhaust fans are both running," her mother explained.

"I was chopping meat," Wendy's father added. (He was the master chef.) "We couldn't hear anything."

"Western music sounds alike," Grandmother mumbled.

"I thought we all knew the Chinese national anthem: 'Arise, people who would not be slaves.'" Grandfather began to sing, staring intently at Wendy.

"We'll just have to catch the drug dealers another time, Wendy." Her mother was flushed from the stove's heat. She motioned Grandfather to stop singing. "We have to get ready for our dinner with Mr. Lee tonight."

"Hey, what's up? What's going on?" Winston was late coming home from his baseball game. He was nine, five years younger than his sister. His straight dark hair was just long enough to stick out from under a brand-new Yankees cap. "Hey, Wendy, why were you playing the national anthem?"

"I'll tell you about it." Wendy looked sullen. "They" — she swept her hand toward her parents and grandparents —

"just messed up the best plan!" Wendy rolled her eyes and proceeded to explain their scheme.

Winston stamped his feet in frustration. "That stinks! Next time, don't you ever leave me out of any intrigue going on in this house!" He wagged an accusing finger at all of them.

~*Chapter* 2~

THAT EVENING, Wendy and Debbie were on-line again.

Dee Sharp reported: *Awesome news! An anonymous informer called the TV station about Eddy's earlobe! Now the police know about the kidnapping.*

Kween Be was quick to respond. *Rocking cool. So what's next? Any leads?*

Can't say. Watch the news. The cops are sure to get lots of tips. Rumors are already flying that he's being hidden in some beach house on Long Island or Queens. The best part is, no one knows the Chins are illegal. Thank the Ancestors!

Wow, how like James Bond! Truly rad! I miss Chinatown.

Know the really best part? People here will feel like part of New York City for a change, Dee Sharp added. *Get this: Mrs. Chin showed my mom the piece of flesh when she came to ask for donations. Mom said it was brown and black and looked like a piece of dried bean cake! Then the cops took some of Eddy's clothing and sent the piece of flesh to some lab for DNA testing.*

Great. Now we can chill.

Not yet. I'm too wired in.

What do you mean? asked Kween Be.

It's just so uncool to chill when everyone is all wired in. Anyway, how's life uptown?

Wendy demurred. *Nothing so exciting. Oh, my God, you don't know what I'm going through! I still haven't made a single friend in school.*

Debbie was surprised. *So why not? You're an honor student and totally cool.*

Maybe in Chinatown I'm cool. But here I'm a nerd.

That's sick! Are you for real?

Wendy lamented. *Yeah, for sure. I saw some Asian faces, but two turned out to be Japanese. They're shy and look just like my friends in Chinatown. When I asked if I could invite them home after school, Grandma said I should ignore them or she would disown me!!!*

That freaks me out. What gives?

Freaks me out, too. Kween Be nodded her head off screen. *Grandma told me some gruesome stories of how the Japanese did terrible stuff to the Chinese. She called it "The Chinese Holocaust." I think it happened during World War II, but she talks as if everything happened yesterday.*

Yeah, my mom's the same. She goes ballistic when people lump her with the Japs. Totally rad.

I'm trying the Koreans in school, Kween Be announced. *But their English! They get the* l *and* r *sounds mixed up, like "Are you leady for runch" Can you believe it?*

No way. That's too weird.

Well, maybe I'll check them out anyway. Come to think of it, they sound just like my grandpa. He also gets the l *and* r *sounds mixed up.*

Your grandpa is old. These girls are young! Duh!

There's this one Chinese girl. From Hong Kong, I think. She's a real label hanger. All she ever wears is Tommy Hilfiger or Ralph Lauren. Don't know what to make of her.

Seriously? Why are you still looking for Asian friends? Haven't you seen enough Chinese faces in Chinatown? You said your great-great-grandfather came to America to build the railroad, so you belong. Don't you?

Wendy loved Debbie's spunkiness. Debbie had come to the United States when she was ten. Now she spoke like a New Yorker, without a Chinese accent. Sometimes she acted more American than Wendy.

Debbie's family lived in Chinatown, and they owned a laundry in Greenwich Village.

Wendy replied: *Oh, sure, it's easy for you to say. Your parents learned English in Hong Kong — they were so Westernized.*

Grandpa always cooked in Chinatown. He never had to say two words to an American.

Wendy knew Debbie had never studied American history in her grade school in Hong Kong.

Grandma and Grandpa don't trust white people because in the old days, American laws did not allow Chinese families here.

Still, it's totally cool to be a fifth-generation American like you.

Yeah, right! Grandpa was always part of the Chinatown all-male bachelor society. Get this: He sent all his savings to China and went back there every ten or twelve years to try to make his wife pregnant!! Dad was born there.

Seriously? Sick! You never told me that.

Yeah, sick all right. When Grandpa retired, he went back to Shamchun Village and bought a bit of land. <L.O.L.> On screen, Wendy laughed out loud.

So how come you were born here?

Wendy blinked from the glare of the computer monitor, but she typed on. *Check this out: Since Grandpa was a citizen, Dad was born an American in China. <B.G.> But he did not know a word of English when he first came to the United States. So naturally, he cooked and — would you believe it? — he also sent all his money "home," to China.*

That's weird, and so unreal. But you still didn't say how you were born here.

Eat your heart out! Remember talking about the Chinese Cultural Revolution in our Chinese history class? The Communists were killing capitalists and foreign spies. So my "American" grandparents had to come back to New York. They finally stopped sending money to China and kept their savings in America. Now they call Chinatown home! Later, my parents married and opened the House of Wong. This is the first time we've ever lived outside Chinatown.

Wendy rose to stretch. She felt quite tired, but decided to wait for Debbie's response.

Can't wait to visit your new place! Try meeting some real Americans. It'll be awesome! I mean, are you really Chinese? Like, you've never even been to China!

Give me a break! I've never even been outside the city.

A lotta people say New York is not really a part of America.

So what am I? Kween Be asked.

A Noo Yawker, of course! <L.O.L.>

The restaurant's not even ready yet. There's still dust, <C.O.L.> (coughing out loud), and noise from the construction. Besides, Mr. Lee told us about the druggies loitering around. Guess what? I'll be playing an important part trying to catch them. :)

Wendy just couldn't help telling her friend everything. She wrote about the plan the family had devised, and how her first attempt to sound the alarm had been a complete flop.

God, Wendy, somebody wake me! You guys really doing this? Rockin' rad!

You bet! <B.G.> Move over James Bond.

This is either incredibly awesome or uncool — I don't know which. I can't believe you're not calling the cops! Maybe someone could report it for you?

Wendy suddenly wondered if Debbie had been the anonymous caller who had informed the TV station about Eddy's kidnapping.

Wendy shot back to explain their unusual predicament: *Mr. Lee said the police already knew. Our building had been empty for over a year, and there's the alley under my window, which is hard to patrol. They can't do much about it.*

Debbie was momentarily dismayed. *With your parents, grandparents, and Leaky Boots mixed up in all this, you can forget about playing James Bond. Anyway, do you think we can meet up sometime? I really do miss you.*

Wendy was quick to return the kindness. *That's sweet. We should try getting together in Central Park sometime. How about this weekend? Maybe we can cruise around the park and get some fresh air. The traffic on First Avenue is just as bad as in Chinatown, so I'll need some peace and quiet. Talk to you tomorrow — same time. :)*

Wendy sat down to do her homework. She went to bed early, exhausted from all the talk about Eddy's kidnapping and her family's plans to catch drug dealers.

Overhead, the whirling helicopter drones louder and louder. It swerves to the left, missing the rocks that jut over her by inches. Suddenly, it is charging directly toward her. Machine guns spray bullets everywhere. Clouds of smoke, sand, grass, and broken stones swirl all around her. Boom! Bombs are exploding.

"Take cover, take cover!" she shouts to Eddy, who is screaming and covering his ears. Wendy runs and sweeps Eddy into her arms. She throws herself under the overhanging rocks, cuddling little Eddy underneath. She hides among the wet grass. She feels the earth quaking beneath her and Eddy shivering and whimpering beside her. Her heart races. Fear chokes her throat, and she pants for air. Bang! The overshadowing rocks are cracking up, one by one. . .

Wendy screamed. She threw back her blanket and leaped from her bed, this time panting for real. The sunlight of a February morning brought reality back in a flood. A pneumatic drill crackled like gunfire downstairs, where teams of workers from Chinatown had arrived at seven. The House of Wong was rattling its way toward a grand opening in May. For almost a week now, the construction workers had been turning the gray limestone facade into red beams and golden dragons — a dwelling fit for an emperor.

Wendy's parents and grandparents were proud of this radical transformation, remarking that the House of Wong would be a landmark on First Avenue. Now, along with forever reminding the kids to set a good example so the family could "carry much face" in the community, Grandpa never ceased to lecture about how the youngsters represented the Chinese People, and how they must make all the Chinese proud in front of the "foreigners."

"But I'm a native-born American!" Wendy would retort.

"You'll always be Chinese," Grandma would reply.

"Well, I'm American Chinese!"

"That's what you may think. If your schoolmates are proud of you, then you'll be Chinese American."

Wendy did feel different in her new private school. For one thing, she was a partial scholarship student, and she had to work especially hard to maintain her grade point average and set a good example. She appreciated the challenges of her new environment, but she hated the construction noise and the daily atmosphere of semi-chaos. Stuffing cotton balls into her ears, she stretched, yawned, and began dressing.

In the dining room, the family was settling around the table. Wendy's mother and grandmother served steaming bowls of soft, gluey rice seasoned with scallions, ginger, and slivers of raw fish fillet — Grandmother's favorite breakfast.

At the House of Wong on Canal Street in Chinatown, meals were served from the restaurant kitchen. The family lived upstairs. Every morning, Wendy could order any number of breakfast items: steamed buns filled with roast pork or mushrooms and vegetables; chicken or beef stir-fried noodles; dumplings stuffed with seasoned meats or shrimps; or vegetables neatly wrapped in crescents and circles of rice or wheat flour dough. She could skip the Western-style lunch served in her school and come home in the afternoon for a snack of savory leftovers. Now, Grandmother's daily fare — soupy rice accompanied by fried dough sticks, salted duck eggs, black "thousand-year-old-eggs," and peanuts — left her feeling hollow by lunchtime. Since moving uptown, she had to buy lunch at school. Although unaccustomed to American food, Wendy had developed a special fondness for spaghetti and pizza.

Winston slurped down his bowl of rice and grabbed a handful of peanuts as he excused himself from the table. His smooth round face and little globular nose were still gleaming from the steam that rose from the hot boiled rice.

"Bye, everyone. Gotta run, or I'll be late for practice!" Winston hollered as he ran for the door.

Grandfather waylaid him. "Here, Wai Kuo." (The grandparents always addressed the children by their Chinese names.)

"Some more peanuts for you." He stuffed another handful of peanuts into Winston's trouser pocket and patted him on the Yankees cap.

"Thanks, Grandpa." Winston winked at the smiling wrinkled face and flowing white beard. He knew that amid the peanuts would be a pack of chewing gum, of which his mother and grandmother disapproved.

Wendy munched on the fried dough sticks, savoring the warm, sticky morsels as they made their way into her stomach. For a moment she forgot the banging noise from downstairs. The sound of whirling drills and clanging metals grew fainter when the family shared breakfast and carried on their loud morning conversations.

"The weather has been so pleasant that the workers can surely finish framing the storefront this week," Mr. Wong shouted over the construction din. He lifted his arms and formed the shape of a doorframe to demonstrate. The family had become so used to raising their voices that no one noticed the exaggerated gestures.

"Yes, soon we'll have a grand opening," said Grandma with a nod. She took a long, slow slurp and sucked in her soupy rice. Wendy looked away. She wondered what her new school friends would think of her foreign grandma.

"Wendy, I heard you scream this morning," Wendy's mother said, smacking her lips as she chewed on the marinated thousand-year-old egg. "Did you wake up from a bad dream?"

Wendy nearly choked on a peanut. The runny black egg yolk smeared on her mother's lips, and pieces of glassy brown egg white sparkled through her mother's teeth. Their uptown neighbors would find this sight revolting, Wendy thought. In Chinatown she would be disgusted to see Chinese diners sucking fish and chicken and throwing, and sometimes even spitting, the bones right on the table. At least her family placed the bones in dishes and kept the tables clean. Still, her stomach turned whenever she saw her family savoring food that was simply gross! Grandpa had written an ode to braised duck feet, and Grandma always raved about her favorite soup, chicken feet simmered with mushrooms. Wendy sighed. Someone had to tell them that those dishes would never sell in an uptown restaurant. It was impossible to imagine her family integrated into the neighborhood. She lowered her head and coughed. "I . . . I thought I was late getting up this morning." She drew her mouth into the shape of a small heart, and brought her hands up to finger on an imaginary flute. She blurted out: "I have orchestra practice . . ."

She faltered in midsentence. The silence downstairs enveloped the dining room so suddenly that she felt herself shouting and playing a clownlike mime at the same time. Everyone stopped eating. After the thunder of construction noise, the clatter of the family laying down its chopsticks resounded like a cascade of tumbling logs.

"What's going on?" Wendy's father asked, pushing back his chair with a loud scraping sound. Below, a door slammed, and a pair of running feet pounded on the wooden stairs. A breathless worker burst into the family dining room.

"Mr. Wong, Mr. Wong! You've been served with a Stop Work Order!"

~*Chapter 3*~

WENDY STOOD BY the stairs. Her grandparents were staring at the two tall men in khaki pants and down jackets. They pointed and mumbled in Chinese about these "foreign devils" bringing trouble. The men waved an official-looking form in front of Mr. Wong, shouting: "Construction must stop! You have been red-tagged!"

Ignoring the threat, her mother smiled and bowed to no one in particular. "Come up for some tea. It is a mess down here." Wendy wanted to drop dead from embarrassment watching her mother kowtow and pretend that this was just a social visit.

"No, thanks," came the curt response from the sandy-haired man with watery blue eyes. He seemed the gentler of the two, a half-smile curled around his thin lips. His dark-haired companion flicked his index finger at the Stop Work Order, and barked loudly over everyone's heads: "The local Community Board lodged this complaint. They want to stop the roaches from Chinatown!" Seeing the effect he was having on his cowed listeners, he smirked on: "They don't want to degrade their neighborhood."

"No deglade, no deglade," her father bowed fawningly. When agitated, he would forget his English grammar and revert to his thick Chinese accent. Wendy got a sinking feeling whenever she heard her normally proud father adopt this servile tone.

"We'll have to inspect the premises for cockroaches and other violations," the sandy-haired man drawled. Wendy didn't like his smile.

"No ploblem, no ploblem. . . . Everyone eat the house and get flee gift! When we open . . ." Mr. Wong bowed again.

Wendy could not bear to watch. Her discomfort was quickly developing into tears. Grandma nudged her toward the door. "Go to school," she whispered.

Wendy obeyed. Even if she had wanted to stay, she could not be late for orchestra. This year the school's spring concert would feature the famous folk tune "Greensleeves." All the flutists in school would be auditioning for the solo part. The orchestra would also play in the production of *Fiddler on the Roof,* and a flutist would be chosen to perform a duet with the violin in the overture. Wendy had been practicing extra hard.

Anyway, it was unthinkable that Wendy would skip school for even one day. When the family moved from Canal Street, Wendy and Winston were told in no uncertain terms that it was for their benefit. Too many new immigrants in Chinatown were struggling with the English language, just like the adults in the Wong household; the children needed to be immersed in English.

Their wise friend Mr. Lee, whose shop was located a few blocks away on Lexington Avenue, told them that the public schools on the Upper East Side used to be the best in New York. The grade schools were still fine, but some of the high schools were now run like armed camps. Security guards checked for weapons and drugs at the entrance. Some of these schools even had daycare centers for unmarried teenage mothers. Without mincing words, Mr. Lee told them that private schools were the best option. When Wendy won a partial scholarship to attend a prestigious private school, the family moved. Now, Wendy's grades and exemplary behavior must pave the way for Winston's scholarship when it was time for him to enter high school.

Wendy remembered the steady drone of parents and grandparents impressing this immense responsibility upon her — how the future of the family depended upon the children's education. She wanted to object to the burden placed upon the whole family, and the big changes everyone would have to make. But deep down, she was proud and also fascinated by the possibilities in the uptown world. Wendy knew that the outside world of white people remained a total mystery to her family. If only Debbie could move with her, then she could help her family become truly American.

The troubles at home shadowed Wendy all day. She had been there for only a few weeks. Everyone in school acted normally, talking and laughing. Could any of them even imagine what was going on in her house? True, she had often told Debbie that sometimes she was embarrassed by her family. But no one deserved to go through all this. Whenever she thought of that morning's scene, she had to choke back tears; later, during recess, she would run to the bathroom and cry.

She knew her parents and grandparents were puzzled by the objections raised by their new neighbors. Forget even trying to integrate her family into the new neighborhood. The new neighbors had already rejected them. Did this Stop Work Order mean a delay or a shutdown? Would they have to move back to Chinatown? They had already sold the restaurant on Canal Street. Without a restaurant, how was the family going to make a living? Wendy thought she was lucky to be out of Chinatown, but this was worse, much worse!

Wendy went to the audition in a state of confusion. Dozens of violinists and flutists swarmed around the rehearsal room, tuning up and practicing tricky trills and spiraling passages. Chaotic noises skittered across the room, adding to her sense of dismay. She did not bother to greet anyone but went straight into a corner to practice and warm up. When it was her turn to play for the music teachers and the conductor, she channeled all her anguish and dark worries into the music. Her high notes soared into longing, and her low notes moaned for understanding. Totally immersed in the music's eloquence, she fingered and blew in her practiced way. Gradually, the tight knots in her throbbing heart began to loosen. A young man outside the audition room told her afterward, "That was so cool, very expressive. I felt like I saw shadows when you played."

Wendy smiled in gratitude, but quickly lowered her head. She felt hot, and her face flushed. Was it because of the exertion of the competition, or was she surprised by this unexpected kindness? Her heart started to thump in her chest.

"We've never met. Are you new here?" The young man smiled. He moved his bow to his left hand, where he had his violin tucked under his armpit. He extended his right hand. "I'm David DiVario, a senior. I'm waiting for my turn to play the solo part in the *Fiddler.*"

Wendy mumbled her name, barely touching David's hand to shake it. "Yes, I'm new here. I'm a freshman."

"Did you say Wendy Wong?" his eyes widened. "We're double, double!"

"What? Oh, you mean . . ."

"Awesome!" David smiled into her eyes. "I mean I'm double *D,* and you're double *W.*" He tilted his head, bringing his face to her eye level.

Wendy could not help laughing. Blushing furiously and not knowing how to respond, she nodded. Would she have answered with something light and funny at her old school? Probably not. Debbie, who always seized the moment, might have emulated David's flirtation by saying, "Rad, wow. So should we try going out as a double-double?" Wendy's parents and grandparents, on the other hand, had told her repeatedly that a Chinese girl must be modest and should never, ever be too forward. Wendy pulled on her poker face. Mumbling her thanks and excuses all in a rush, she turned to place her flute in its case and ran to her next class.

Oh, what a jerk I am! I should have been friendlier, she thought. *David's brown eyes look sincere. And he may be worried about playing well. I could have talked about the friendly judges and calmed his fears. He is awfully cute. Yet the two men bringing the Stop Work Order this morning also looked like they could have been gentlemen under different circumstances. Appearances don't mean anything,* she warned herself.

Later, as she was walking by the principal's office, she noticed David DiVario's name on the Honor Roll board. *So, he is an achiever also,* she thought. *Is he here on a scholarship? Does he know that I am? Well, that doesn't matter. I wish I had told him how nervous I was, and how kind the music teachers are. I could have shared some of my Zen wisdom. Told him that once you started playing, the time flew. That might have helped him be at ease at the competition. I should have wished him good luck, at least. Sick! A fine debut for Kween Be. Well, now it's too late.* She sighed.

All in a daze, she plodded through the rest of the day. In spite of the bustle in school, she felt separate from the others. As Wendy trudged home in her new neighborhood, her head ached; her limbs felt heavy, her chest tight, and her palms sweaty. Although she had been born in New York City and never lived anyplace else, now she was in a truly different world, up here on First Avenue. She was used to the crowded, narrow streets of Chinatown: the jumble of neon signs, rich colors, and ornate decorations on doors, banners, and shop windows. There, billowing Technicolor designs obscured the old brick and gray stone buildings. Even the old telephone booths were crowned with small pagoda roofs.

Oh, how Wendy missed the pungent smells! Restaurants, grocery stores, and bakeries lined every street. Wendy's mouth watered when she walked past the delicatessen window displaying rows of roasted pork, chickens, and ducks. The tantalizing smell of anise seed, curried squid, soy sauce, and drying vegetables spelled home on every corner. Itinerant hawkers peddled their goods along the main avenues: umbrellas, watches, shirts, shoes, and other colorful merchandise. People hailed each other with hearty warmth, speaking the many different dialects of China. The Wongs were old-timers in Chinatown, and most people knew who she was.

Now, walking down First Avenue, she was greeted by the impersonal hubbub of constant traffic. The strident horns, wailing ambulances, and howling police cars punctuated the steady drone of tires whooshing down the asphalt. People floated by without recognizing her. They strode by the fancy windows, stopped to gaze for a moment, and went in or continued on their way. She felt so insignificant amid the staunch gray buildings. The opulent designer-clothing shops looked foreign. The art galleries were off-putting. Even the occasional restaurant felt alien.

A gusty wind tunneled down the avenue, sweeping her long straight hair over her face. As the dusty sunlight filtered through its dark strands, she had an ethereal feeling, like being in a cathedral. People strode by with grim, closed faces. No wonder her grandparents thought them ghostlike. Wendy used to bristle when her grandparents called all Caucasians "foreign devils" or "foreign ghosts." In fact, she had often rolled her eyes and sputtered: "C'mon, guys, don't you realize they see us as foreigners in this country?"

"Ah-yah, anyone who not know our fine culture is foreigner and a barbarian." Grandma would shake her finger and reply with certainty.

In Chinatown, Wendy could read the faces of all her friends. More often than not they wore graphic expressions of their fears and joys. Mimi liked to emphasize the maudlin. Debbie was inclined to be melodramatic, and Jason always seemed ecstatic. Now, she was inclined to agree with her grandmother: The closed faces were truly ghostlike.

Walking with hair streaming down her face, Wendy caught a glimpse of two people lurking in the alleyway next to her family's restaurant. *Are they doing drugs? Smoking pot? Planning a crime?* Her steps quickened. She turned to take a better look, but bumped into a short, stout woman who was rolling up her awning. Wendy dropped her flute case.

"Excuse me!" Wendy gasped. She picked up the case.

"Oh . . . you gave me such a start!" The woman lowered a plump little hand over her heart. "I'm Emily Horton. I own this bookstore. Are you the young lady next door who plays the flute?"

"Yes, Mrs. Horton," Wendy answered in a small voice. She noticed a gold wedding ring. *I must look like a wreck,* she thought. *What a terrible impression I'm making!* "I'm Wendy Wong." As the weather had been unseasonably warm, she had practiced the flute with her windows open. She asked if her music had annoyed anyone.

"Oh, your music lifts me out of my blues." Mrs. Horton's hazel eyes twinkled reassuringly. She ran her fingers through her mop of short, curly gray hair. Looking at Wendy she remarked, "My, what lovely long, flowing hair!"

"Er . . . thanks." Wendy's eyes glowed with surprise. She wanted to say more, but words eluded her.

"This awning is just impossible in the wind." Mrs. Horton dropped her arms, ready to give up.

"I'll give you a hand. But first I'll just drop off my books."

Smiling, Wendy ran into the restaurant. Grandpa was just coming to greet her when she saw his mouth drop open in a soundless shout, his face white. A loud crash came from the plate glass window behind her. She heard Mrs. Horton scream, "Stop! Stop those men!"

Wendy swung around and saw a gaping crack in the front window. Shock, anger, fear, and bewilderment swept over her in a flash. "What . . . what happened?" Her voice trembled.

Grandpa grabbed Wendy's arm. He leaned on her, panting uncontrollably. His eyes became two pools of crystals, and his face turned so red; all the blood must have rushed to it. "Someone . . . some person threw a stone, a rock, maybe a bottle." He pointed to the window, and his whole body shook.

Mrs. Horton rushed in. "Are you all right? I saw these two men run by the restaurant and throw something." Mrs. Horton put a hand around Wendy's shoulder. She would have embraced Wendy if Wendy hadn't been carrying a backpack and supporting Grandpa on her arms.

"I'm . . . we're not hurt," Wendy whispered, her heart racing as if she had been running a marathon. "But I should bring Grandpa upstairs."

Mrs. Horton stared at Wendy's red-faced grandfather and wrung her hands. "Let me help you bring him up."

In the next moment, Grandma and Wendy's parents all rushed downstairs. Their eyes bulged as they surveyed the scene of destruction. Their mouths hung open to shrieks of shock that shattered the dusty air.

"I live next door. I must call the police. I'll be right back." Mrs. Horton nodded to all the Wongs and ran out.

"What happened? What happened?" sputtered Wendy's family. They hovered around Grandpa.

"I was facing inside. I didn't see what happened," Wendy tried to explain. She could not keep the tremor from her voice.

Grandpa was not much help either. "One man . . . several men . . . ran by and . . . and threw something . . . a stone. The woman said something. Everything happened so . . . so fast . . . it was all a blur. Then . . . over there . . . too much glare from the window."

"So much debris outside — how can we know what was thrown?" Wendy's father mumbled.

"The glass did not shatter!" Grandma cried and held on to her husband's hand. The two of them huddled together, trembling. "Thank the Buddha you're not hurt!" Her palm rose to her heart, and she pressed and soothed her chest, then she bent toward her husband and pressed and swirled her hand around and around his chest as well. Meanwhile the cacophony of moans, sighs, exclamations of fear, and yelps of outrage sent Wendy into more confusion.

"But who do you think did this?" Wendy hugged and steeled herself. Her face felt hot, and she knew it must have turned crimson.

"Do you think this is another 'message' from the Community Board?" Wendy's mother whispered in terror; her ashen face turned away from the light.

"It'll take another fortune to repair this window." Grandma's voice wavered.

"The insurance will replace the window, Ma!" Wendy's father tried to sound calm. He balled his hands into fists and stood very still. "Perhaps the woman next door saw the person doing the throwing. Do you know her?" He looked at Wendy. His question made Wendy's heart skip a beat.

"When I came home from school, I met Mrs. Horton outside." Wendy grimaced. "I was coming in to drop off my books so I could help her take down her awning."

Mr. Wong wiped his forehead, despite the cool temperature in the room. "Do you know if Mrs. Horton is on the Community Board?"

"All I know is that she's gone to call the police." Wendy felt angry all of a sudden. "Give me a break, for goodness' sake. I hardly know her."

Was the family under attack? Who had thrown what, and did someone order the vandalism? Wendy gripped her books and turned rigid.

"Grandma and I, I . . . I will help Grandpa upstairs." Wendy's mother slurred her words as if she had been drinking. "Wendy, stay with your Dad and wait for the police."

Soon Mrs. Horton returned. "This is Officer Hogan, and I am Emily Horton." She introduced herself to Mr. Wong, offering her hand. He touched the hand with hardly a grip and let it slip immediately. He nodded and tried to smile. Unaccustomed to talking to a policeman, he turned mute.

"Hi." Wendy lowered her head. Again she was overcome by confusion.

"Officer Hogan." Mrs. Horton turned to the patrolman. "Meet my new neighbors: Wendy Wong and Mr. Wong."

Officer Hogan tipped his hat. "I'm terribly sorry to see this happen to your new place. Let's see if we can get to the bottom of this."

"Mrs. Horton, did you see who threw the bottle or stone?" Wendy had found a quivering voice.

"No! I saw two men . . . around six feet tall, I'd say . . . wearing dark sweatshirts with hoods over their heads. It's so windy I didn't think anything of it. Then, bang! One of them threw something, and both of them ran flying down the street.

I screamed as loud as I could, but I really didn't get a good look at their faces."

"Were there other people on the street?" Officer Hogan asked.

"Not many." Mrs. Horton frowned. "It was just too windy. Most people were all bundled up and probably didn't hear me. No one ran after those men."

"You know, Mr. Wong, that alley is a hot spot for druggies," Officer Hogan informed them. "I'm so glad you folks are moving in. Maybe your customers will drive away all the mischief around here."

"I hope so." Mr. Wong nodded.

"Did you see anything, Miss?" The officer looked at Wendy.

"No, I was facing inside when I heard Mrs. Horton scream." Wendy decided not to mention her grandfather's presence. Grandpa was already in shock. Being questioned by the police might rattle him further. Officer Hogan seemed so friendly, and he looked as if he had things under control. Shouldn't she be telling him about the drug sniffing and possible assassination plot she had overheard in her room? *Not now*, she thought. The neighbors had already filed a Stop Work Order. They would not appreciate more news of possible criminal activities taking place near the restaurant.

She glanced quickly toward her father, but he was busy examining some forms Officer Hogan had given him. He would need to file them with his insurance company. Her father kept nodding while the officer mumbled his instructions. She wondered if he understood everything.

"We'll do our best to catch those vandals!" Officer Hogan bowed awkwardly to the three of them and again tipped his hat. "Well, good day to you all." He walked out without so much as mentioning the Stop Work Order.

Mr. Wong stood there with a frozen smile and fumbled with the forms while Wendy still clutched her books and carried her backpack. She knew that her father would consult Mr. Lee about the forms. Perhaps they would need her to translate. She had no experience with legal documents. She would have to use a dictionary and figure things out as best she could.

Mrs. Horton smiled at Mr. Wong. "Don't you worry about this anymore, Mr. Wong. I'm sure Officer Hogan will be patrolling our street more frequently now."

"Yes, thank you." Wendy's father nodded politely.

Mrs. Horton turned to Wendy. "As I remember, you were coming in to drop off your books and help me with my awning? Still interested?"

"Oh, of course," Wendy answered quickly. She was glad to have this diversion, though the sight of her father's bloodshot eyes and frozen smile was unnerving. "Dad, are you all right?"

"Yes, yes. Go help her." Her father nodded, tapping the police forms against his free hand as if they were junk mail. A nest of weary lines seemed to have sprung up around his watery eyes. He trudged upstairs.

Wendy immediately dropped off her backpack and books. Running outside again and working with Mrs. Horton somehow calmed her.

"The design of your front door is so interesting." Mrs. Horton pointed next door as she worked. "It's clever the way you recessed the facade. I like that outdoor shaded foyer. Who was your architect?"

"An architect from Chinatown; my parents and grandparents all sort of decided together."

Wendy took down the frame support for the awning while Mrs. Horton rolled up the canvas. She was grateful that Mrs. Horton had pulled her mind away from the latest shock. She did not mention that the architect from Chinatown was a distant relative, also fresh off the boat, and that the true architect of the restaurant was the geomancer, or the "wind-and-water" man.

Before any important decisions were made, her grandparents always consulted this feng-shui expert, who read and interpreted visible and invisible signs of positive and negative forces in the landscape. Her grandparents believed that cosmic powers permeated the environment. In their minds, the position and placement of every door and window must allow free circulation of life forces that will lead to a productive, happy life. Their feng-shui man had recommended that the front door be tilted toward the south, from where he saw great fortune flowing toward the family.

"They are very clever indeed!" Mrs. Horton rolled up the canvas. "Until today, I had not met any member of your family."

"Oh, they're busy with our restaurant, and every day, they visit old friends in Chinatown." In spite of her self-consciousness, Wendy turned to stare at Mrs. Horton. *What a kind woman,* she thought. *She must be about Grandma's age.* She knew her grandparents would never come out to meet this "Guailo — Foreign Devil." The Stop Work Order this morning, and now the rock thrown at the window, would strengthen their ancient fears that the Chinese were unwelcome guests, and that the American Chinese would be foolish to act as if they were equal citizens.

"Officer Hogan has been on this beat for over ten years." Mrs. Horton smiled. "He is a good sort, a real old-fashioned, courtly gentleman."

"Well, I hope that means he'll come by here more often. He might scare away some of the . . . bad people." Wendy remembered the horror on Grandpa's face. She pulled herself up straight and tried to smile back.

"I'll tell him to come here and listen to your flute playing," Mrs. Horton said with a mischievous glint in her eyes. "Can you play 'Danny Boy'? I know he'll love it!"

"Yeah, sure, I know that tune." *Oh, cool. Maybe I can help!* "I do hope he'll come and listen," she said aloud. "I usually practice after doing some homework. Around four-thirty."

"Great, I'll tell him." Mrs. Horton winked, tidying up her awning. "Thanks for helping. Do you think your folks might recommend books with a Chinese point of view? I'd love to stock some in my store." Mrs. Horton said this with a wistful grin, looking deep into Wendy's eyes.

"Sure, my mom has tons of books. She's always reading." *Mother might enjoy meeting Mrs. Horton, and the family would get to know some neighbors. The family needs help, and we are at our best when serving dinner to our guests.* Suddenly inspired, she blurted out: "If you and your husband — "

"I'm a widow, and I live alone."

"Oh." Wendy widened her eyes, but somehow managed to stutter her invitation: "Well, if . . . if you're free, why don't you come and have dinner with us tonight? We usually eat at around six-thirty."

"I had planned on waiting for the restaurant to open before I came to dinner, but it looks as if you'll be delayed. So I accept." Mrs. Horton chuckled with delight.

Wendy's thoughts came in a flurry. *She knows the restaurant cannot open. Maybe she knows about the Stop Work Order? I wonder if she is one of those people who signed the complaint, or if she is a member of the Community Board who wants to come and inspect for cockroaches. She looks so confident — just like an activist! How can I have invited her for dinner?* An ominous frown replaced the dimpled smile on Wendy's face, and she began to feel as if she had asked a viper into her home. What had prompted her to issue such an invitation anyway? *Mrs. Horton certainly tried to help and comfort us,* Wendy reasoned. *Somehow, I don't feel threatened by the way she handles everything. So maybe I have done the right thing.*

Without the workers, the restaurant was a deserted ruin. Wendy picked her way carefully past the cut plasterboards, wood beams, nails, and piles of debris. She examined the cracked window and ran upstairs to the family quarters.

She found the family gathered around the dining table.

"Now we must select a lawyer to help us file these insurance forms and fight the Stop Work Order," Mr. Wong was saying.

"This is not Chinatown. We are not dealing with the Chinese," her mother was quick to point out. "We'll have to hire a foreign ghost lawyer!" Her voice sounded more shrill and nervous than her calm demeanor suggested.

"Foreign devils are always more expensive," Wendy's grandmother spurted out, pointing an accusing finger at her daughter-in-law.

"We have already gone into debt buying this place," Grandfather remarked, sipping his tea to calm his agitation.

"You are all correct, of course." Her father's voice cracked. "We don't even know any foreign ghost lawyer that we can trust." He rose from his chair and paced the floor.

"Get this. I've invited Mrs. Horton from next door to dinner tonight," Wendy announced with as much sprightly enthusiasm as she could muster. "Perhaps she could help you with the forms, and you could ask her about a lawyer?"

"Can't trust a foreign woman. I'll ask Mr. Lee to help," Mr. Wong asserted.

"C'mon, Dad, you saw how friendly she was. Grandpa, are you all right?"

"Wai Weh, I'm fine." Grandfather gave Wendy a look of impatience. "We have already lost so much face. This is no time to be hobnobbing with our neighbors!" He continued to worry his wispy beard.

"I wouldn't be surprised if the same neighbors who sent us the Stop Work Order also sent people to throw things. Maybe Mrs. Horton is one of them!" her grandmother hissed.

"No. Mrs. Horton seemed very concerned when she introduced Officer Hogan," Mr. Wong mused.

Wendy's mother sat with a rounded back and shoulders slumped forward. Suddenly she straightened herself and looked up with a bright smile. "This is a capital idea! Wendy, how did you think of inviting her? Don't you see? We can learn something from this foreign woman." A sudden surge of warmth raced through Wendy.

"Yes, Wendy, that is really good." Mr. Wong came to stand beside her. He turned to address his parents in a soft voice. "Ma and Pa, don't you see? Even if the woman is a troublemaker, we need to find out what's bothering our neighbors. We don't know whether a drug addict threw the stone or if someone hired another person to make mischief."

The grandparents nodded. Having lived as immigrants for so many years, they knew it was often necessary to eat humble pie and make light of losing face. The opposition must be pacified, and they must make a good impression. "Let's clean up this place quickly. And let's ask Mr. Lee to come and bring us some fancy dishes from Chinatown."

Grandma lit more incense for the ancestor tablets, and everyone helped with the cleaning. Even Winston hurried to his room and tidied up his bed and all the baseball paraphernalia he had piled on it. The apartment was still brand new, so within half an hour, the family quarters were spotless. Wendy gave her room a very special inspection, just in case Mrs. Horton was one of those who had signed the complaint about roaches from Chinatown.

I did a very gutsy thing today, she thought. *Mrs. Horton might find us totally unsuitable as neighbors, but she liked my music.* Wendy smiled to herself. *Yes, I'll do some practicing now. That will calm everyone's nerves, and Mrs. Horton will be pleased.*

She took out her music, placed it neatly at the foot of her bed, and opened her flute case. In a flash, she turned and flipped on her computer, sending a message to Debbie:

Lots to tell you tonight at 9:30! — Kween Be.

~*Chapter 4*~

MR. LEE CAME to the apartment at five-thirty, bringing with him a platter of Chinese cold cuts. Edging the round platter, julienned strips of jellyfish glistened in a light brown sauce of vinegar, soy sauce, and toasted sesame oil. The cold cuts in the center formed the shape of a mythical bird. A rooster's head led the way, and white Napa cabbage pickled in a sweet, sour, and hot sauce formed the neck. The body was fashioned out of layers of red roast pork, golden curried squid, brown jellied beef slices, and curls of red marinated shrimp with their shells on. Wendy carried the platter to the refrigerator, her mouth watering.

"Wendy, I heard you're the one who invited the woman who lives next door," Mr. Lee said. "What is she like?"

"I really don't know her very well, Uncle Lee." Mr. Lee was not really a relative, but a polite Chinese child always addressed an adult friend of the family as Uncle or Aunt. Lee Kee Boots, however, was different. He really felt like an uncle. Wendy smiled. "I only met her today. She was so friendly, and I thought she might be able to help."

"Good initiative, Wendy," her father joined in. His face was scrunched up into a frown that seldom left him since he received the Stop Work Order. "But I'm worried that it might be unseemly to ask for help during our first meeting."

"We'll just have to see if she turns out to be a real friend." Mr. Lee sat down, tapping his fingers on the table and snapping his knuckles as if he didn't know what to do with his hands. "Your situation is desperate, after all."

Mrs. Horton arrived shortly after six. She brought a picture book, *A Day in the Life of America.* She held Wendy's grandfather's hands when introduced, and asked repeatedly if he was all right. Grandpa nodded. He did not know how to respond to the stranger's kindly concern, but he was grinning broadly.

Both grandparents smiled and bowed but refrained from speaking. They knew from experience that their poor command of English might create further prejudice. In front of a white person, they behaved like guests, even in their own home. They smiled and nodded constantly, trying to give an impression of being good guests who would not make waves.

Wendy's father introduced Mr. Lee as the owner of Lee Kee Boots on Lexington Avenue.

"Oh, yes!" Mrs. Horton exclaimed. "That's a unique shop. Many of my friends know of it."

"Please come and sit down. Dinner's ready," said Wendy's mother as she led everyone to the table. Wendy helped pour wine for the adults and soda for herself and Winston.

"What a gorgeous dish!" Mrs. Horton said when the mythical bird platter was served. "It is really too beautiful to eat."

"Mr. Lee brought this from Chinatown. We call it the Phoenix Platter. It is supposed to bring good fortune." Mr. Wong nodded his acknowledgment toward Mr. Lee.

"Then we must eat it, mustn't we?" Mrs. Horton chuckled as she tried a piece of the jellied beef. "Ah, a five-spice sauce. Delicious!"

"So you're familiar with Chinese food," Mr. Lee responded with obvious pleasure.

"Wo kan tar tze dau" (I can see she understands), said Grandma. "She handles her chopsticks like one of us."

"Oh, I love Chinese food with a passion." Mrs. Horton shelled the shrimp expertly with her teeth like a Chinese, and did not seem bothered by the spicy Napa cabbage. "I used to go to Chinatown once a week to get genuine Chinese food, though I'm never sure if I'm ordering the right things."

"You didn't find Chinatown dirty or ugly?" Mr. Lee stole a sidelong glance at Mrs. Horton.

"Oh, no!" Mrs. Horton answered, balancing a piece of curried squid on her chopsticks. "There is a certain charm in eating food in a natural and earthy way. Plus, the cuisine is a lot more authentic than some of those phony Chinese restaurants one sees uptown, even if they are more elegant."

Wendy almost shouted with glee. The rigidly smiling faces around the table softened.

"Did you ever try the fish stomachs in Chinatown?" Winston teased.

"You didn't mind eating the chicken and duck feet?" Wendy couldn't help blurting out after Winston. She felt her mother's pinch on her thigh under the table. Their father shot a withering glare.

"Oh, I never ordered those items." Mrs. Horton laughed. "Like most Americans, I enjoy our familiar meats and vegetables cooked in your exotic ways. Now I particularly enjoy many different varieties of Chinese vegetables, including the bitter melon! Many in my gourmet club love the French way of preparing goose livers, but I never developed the taste."

Wendy wanted to tell Mrs. Horton that she and Winston also never developed the taste for many organ meats and unusual cuts that the Chinese savor. But instead she bit on her lower lip and gave her mother a knowing nod.

"The House of Wong aims to present authentic Chinese food, no compromise," Mr. Wong said.

"But we will become . . . achieve . . . er, how do you say it? Real uptown sophistication," her mother added confidently. She pronounced each word slowly, making sure that her English was correct.

"I'm sure you will, Mrs. Wong. Your daughter tells me you are an avid reader."

"What?" Her mother blushed and lowered her head. Wendy wished she could tell Mrs. Horton that it was considered rude and uncouth for a cultured Chinese to boast of his or her accomplishments. "Oh, my English . . . very poor. I read" — her palms opened up to form a book — "mostly in Chinese."

"Oh." Mrs. Horton sounded a little disappointed. "I understand your English."

"I can read better. My husband, speak slow and good; I speak fast. Can't always . . . remember grammar."

"But you sound very clear."

"I try . . . I try, but no good accent."

"It's all right, so don't worry." Mrs. Horton sighed. "I had mentioned to Wendy that I would love to stock more books that carry a Chinese theme or point of view."

"Oh, I read many books. I do so can in English." Her mother put down her chopsticks, eager to be helpful. "All those stories — about wheeling-dealing Taipans, corrupt officials, and seductive girls. They become . . . so . . . so bestsellers. Fun to read, but tell us not much about Chinese people." She stopped to gauge Mrs. Horton's reaction, uncertain if she was sounding presumptuous or unfair.

Mrs. Horton shook her head. "That's what I suspected."

Emboldened, her mother divulged her opinions in a direct way — not her usual practice in dealing with strangers. "Reporters and university professors more accurate," she continued. "They write books that can be fun to read also."

"Interesting! So you also read scholarly works." Mrs. Horton laid down her chopsticks. She took a sip of her wine and peered closely at the youthful-looking woman in the loose-fitting navy brocade robe.

As the hostess, her mother had chosen to wear a shimmering blue robe embossed with chrysanthemums.

Wendy thought her mother was overdressed, but now she could see the wisdom in her decision. Westerners had such different notions of fashion and elegance. For her mother, however, the robe was more than a fashion statement; it was meant to lend credibility to her person.

"No, no, not many. I try; I try . . . " her mother said.

"Do you have any recommendations, any particular professor or journalist?" Mrs. Horton asked, digging into her food again.

"Oh, no, I'm not reading scholar works."

Wendy knew that to be a Chinese lie. A Chinese woman must appear humble in front of her husband, her in-laws, and such a distinguished family friend as Mr. Lee. In fact, Wendy had seen old books by John King Fairbank, and new books by Iris Chang, Ha Jin, and even the *New York Times* correspondent Nicholas Kristof next to her mother's bed.

"C'mon Mom, Mrs. Horton needs help!" Wendy rolled her eyes in exasperation.

Unwilling to disappoint her guest, her mother diverted her attention to Wendy. "Wendy is a very good reader."

"She likes to cry when she reads!" Winston added.

Now it was Wendy's turn to blush and lower her head. Her heart thumped like a basketball in her chest. She felt cornered, and realized, in a flash, that she had done the same thing to her mother.

By then, everyone around the table, including Mrs. Horton, had stopped eating and was looking at Wendy and her mother.

Exhilarated, not wanting to be left out, Winston piped up again: "Yes, Wendy cried and cried when she read *Little Women* and *David Copperfield*. She said she loved those books. I prefer Harry Potter!"

"I think I know why Wendy likes old stories," her father joined in. "The children in the old days had more responsibilities — like our kids!"

"Actually, I'd like to read more stories about Chinese American teens, like us." Wendy finally found her voice. "So far, I've only been able to find a few books. Many of them are Korean. *Nothing but the Truth* by Justine Chen Headly is good, but even in that book, the heroine is only half Chinese. I can't find anything about people like me who do not lead a tragic family life." She wiped her mouth and quickly served Mrs. Horton a spoonful of Napa cabbage from the platter.

"Thanks for all your input." Mrs. Horton resumed munching. "I must look into all this. By the way, what are these delicious chewy shreds? They give such a flavorful crunch!"

"That is jellyfish, my favorite," Winston answered right away, happy to be helpful and to divert the conversation away from books.

"Grandson, Wai Kuo, when little, call it 'bu-tow, bu-tow' because of this chewing sound." Grandpa's smile showed some of his missing teeth. Wendy noticed that he had changed his mind and had actually spoken in front of this foreign-devil woman. Mrs. Horton's friendliness must have impressed him.

"The House of Wong will be a true asset to our neighborhood," interjected Mr. Lee. "The Wongs have generations of experience. Their food looks good and tastes delicious. They have also mastered the new dimensions of food service: There is proper balance in color, texture, and even the crunchy sounds that stimulate our appetite!"

Everyone was laughing now, and Mrs. Horton raised her wineglass. "A toast, a toast! I was expecting a simple family dinner with my new neighbors, but this is a banquet. I must tell this to the members of my gourmet club — Ambassador Ben Zvi and Judge Bernstein."

The titled names startled the family. "Did they have anything to do with the Stop Work Order?" Wendy's father asked in spite of himself.

"No, on the contrary." Mrs. Horton sipped her wine. "They are devotees of Chinese food. Judge Harry Bernstein is retired, and Mr. Ira Ben Zvi is the Israeli ambassador to the United Nations."

"Do you think your friend the judge might recommend a lawyer to represent us on this problem we have?" Wendy's father diverted his eyes to the ground.

"Oh, I think I could persuade Judge Bernstein to take on the case himself at no cost. He and Ambassador Ben Zvi are both human rights advocates."

Wendy's father looked relieved, but his eyes remained downcast. "I must apologize for my most ungracious behavior when you brought in Officer Hogan to help us. I don't think I even said hello to either of you."

"You must have been in shock, after so many distressing things happened to you. I understand perfectly."

"Are you a member of the Community Board?" Mr. Lee could not help asking.

"No, but I know a few people who are members." Mrs. Horton smiled meaningfully. "You must retain Judge Bernstein and Ambassador Ben Zvi as legal counsel. Their prestige will speak loudly for you. In the meantime, I may be able to help you negotiate a settlement without going to court!"

"Do you think the board sent someone to throw some-thing?" Grandpa whispered in Chinese. Wendy translated.

"I don't think the people on the board would ever approve a thing like that! However, people involved with drugs and other misguided sorts may have dangerous ideas."

"Thank you, thank you!" Grandfather said in English, smiling and nodding.

"Thank you, thank you!" Wendy's father joined in.

Wendy's mother and grandmother started to pile food on Mrs. Horton's plate. Wendy sat back and savored the collective sense of relief that passed through the room. She knew that her grandma would be lighting incense sticks in front of the family ancestor tablets tonight. She would bow and mumble chants of thanksgiving. In her view, the merciful kindness of their ancestors must have sent this new neighbor to guide them in their troubles.

~*Chapter* 5~

THAT EVENING, Wendy frantically pounded away at her computer keyboard.

Too much to tell you tonight — something was thrown through our front window — what's left is a wreck. Everyone is exhausted and has gone to bed. I'll be sitting by the phone. Call me as soon as you can.

After Wendy logged off, Debbie was on the phone, ready to talk. Wendy told her all that had happened that day.

"Sick! Rock throwing? Don't be intimidated — sounds like the work of bullies and cowards! And that Stop Work Order must be totally un-American. It's outrageous!" Debbie fumed.

"Well, we don't know if it was a rock that smashed the window — the workers left some debris outside. After being 'red-tagged' this morning, everyone was already terrified. It's like no one really knows what to do."

"Your family must fight for their rights! Seriously, America is strong because it is a democracy and every citizen has rights. If you want to be a true American, you must fight hard to uphold what's in the Constitution. Don't you know we all have a right to make a living in 'pursuit of happiness'?"

"Of course. You know, you sound like you're quoting from the civic lessons you took for citizenship. My grandparents are never cool. They don't know they have rights, and my parents don't have a clue either. They think consulting Mr. Lee of Leaky Boots fame will teach them everything about being American!"

"I can't believe you're so calm," Debbie said. "This is insane! Seriously, I'd be screaming and pestering that Officer Hogan or something."

"I'm such a dork. I don't know what I'm doing. No one knows what to do." Wendy gulped for air. "This afternoon, I met the woman who owns the bookstore next door. I invited her home for dinner tonight." Wendy told Debbie all about helping Mrs. Horton roll up her awning, the dinner party, and how Mrs. Horton had promised to help them.

"Awesome! See, Wendy, you're not useless."

"Thanks. You can't believe how cool I feel right now. For a while there, I wondered if I'd done the right thing by inviting this total stranger into our home. But as Mr. Lee said, our situation is desperate."

"It is desperate, but also rad in a way, don't you think?"

"Yeah, kind of. I can't tell what my grandparents are thinking. Would you believe this? Tonight Grandma prayed to our ancestors and thanked them for sending us Mrs. Horton."

"That Mrs. Horton sounds cool. I'm sure she liked you."

"Maybe I've learned a thing or two living with grandparents: I feel comfortable with old people. But grandparents are so superstitious!"

"Of course they're superstitious. They may not know any other way to deal with difficult problems."

"I'm still chilled and, like, shaking whenever I think about that rock throwing. Well, anyway, they think it was some kind of stone or rock."

"No difference."

"Yeah, like everyone is holding back, trying not to show their feelings so as not to upset everyone else."

"So uncool!"

"Yeah, my parents haven't brought up the incident even once since it happened."

"Are your parents going to get in touch with that judge and the Israeli ambassador?"

"Oh, I hope so! I know they are happy, like, to get some powerful help through Mrs. Horton, and I hope we'll get to know the community — eventually."

"Awesome, that'll help you fit in. You're so lucky!"

"Maybe, but I don't feel lucky. I just feel like a jerk and start shaking whenever I think about Grandpa."

"Look at things from here. Nothing is happening in Chinatown except that more immigrants with all their problems keep arriving."

"You know, this is the first time I've felt like a fresh-off-the-boat immigrant. Still, you're right. I am lucky in spite of all these horrible things. Let me tell you about this senior I met at the audition."

Wendy told Debbie everything about her meeting with David at the competition.

"Awesome! Can't believe your luck." Debbie was almost breathless now. "This David DiVario sounds really interesting. Try not to mess up. You've got to talk to him again!"

"Do you think I should just, like, walk up to him?"

"Why not? He's probably in orchestra. Can't hurt to say hello and talk about what's happening in school."

"Oh, I don't know."

"Go for it. Look, you already did well for your family. Do you always want to feel like an outsider?

Wendy and Debbie chatted for over an hour. They agreed to meet in Central Park on Sunday morning. When Wendy went to bed, she felt exhilarated. She now knew that she was doing the right things. It had been so reassuring to discuss her adventures with her best friend.

Sunday turned out to be sunny but windy. Gusts of cold air sent debris swirling down the avenues and rattled the ghostly tree branches. The cracking and snapping sounds did not brighten Wendy's mood. She had hoped to show Debbie the Obelisk, walk through the *Alice in Wonderland* sculptures, the Delacorte Theatre, the Turtle Pond, and maybe even take a jog around the reservoir. She had to abandon all such plans. They met at the East Seventy-ninth Street entrance. There were few people in the park. As soon as Wendy saw Debbie, they hugged and headed straight toward the Belvedere Castle, where it was more sheltered. As they leaned against the castle wall, tears streamed down Debbie's face, and Wendy thought the wind must have brought dust into her eyes. "Are you all right? What happened? Did something get into your eyes?" she kept asking.

"Mom and Dad had a big fight last night." Debbie sobbed. "Mom got so mad! She threw the spray bottle for her ironing at Dad. The water bottle knocked Dad's head against the wall, and he started bleeding. Oh, Wendy, it was horrible!" She repeatedly kicked the stone wall.

"Oh, my God, I didn't know your parents do ironing at home too! I thought they're so sophisticated because they know enough English to open a laundry!" Blood rushed into Wendy's face. She stared at her friend's hulking back.

"Yeah, sophisticated all right. They're always talking about money: how to take in more laundry, do more hand ironing for fancy clothes, and save, and save, and save! I'm just so sick of hearing the same things." Her head was so close to the wall that Wendy grabbed her torso and gently nudged her around. Debbie faced Wendy and wiped her face with the back of her hands. Wendy pulled out some tissues.

"Please don't cry," Wendy said, grateful that no one was in the passageway. "My family talks about saving money all the time too. They took on a big mortgage moving uptown."

"Oh, Wendy, let's run away." Debbie's eyes narrowed. "You have hostile neighbors, and my parents worry about the rents going up. They work and work and get nowhere!"

"We have all these problems with the new restaurant, but I thought your parents are cool because they give you piano lessons!" Wendy started weeping too.

"I think poor Mom once wanted to be a musician, so she is always after us about practicing piano. Dad said he is just being practical and wants to sell our old piano. He thinks we're wasting our time! He thinks my sister and I should help with the ironing! Oh, Wendy, let's run away!" Her eyes widened and tears rolled down her face.

"Where can we go?" Wendy wept in earnest. "Both our families seem to be in trouble. My grandparents and sometimes even my parents are so set in their old ways that I often feel like I'm choking. Getting away and being free sounds great! But where can we go? We've never even been outside of New York!"

"Do you have on-line friends?" Debbie's lips curled to into a defiant snarl.

"No, I'm always too busy." Wendy scrunched up her face and exclaimed: "Debbie, you can't be thinking of running to some on-line friend that you don't really know! That is truly dangerous!"

"I know, I know. It could be just some creep on the other end pretending to care for me, but seriously, sometimes I just want to get out of here!" Debbie turned toward the wall again, stamping her feet and kicking the wall.

"Promise me, promise me, Debbie, NEVER, NEVER run away to some unknown creep!" Wendy hugged her friend from behind and pulled her away from the wall.

"I'm not stupid, Wendy." Debbie stopped crying and faced Wendy. "I've read about how some girls get raped and killed when they run to their on-line 'friend.'"

"Don't you have some relatives on the West Coast?"

"My aunt lives in San Francisco, but if I go there, I'll just be sent back and Mom will be devastated."

Wendy chewed her lip. She realized that she must not agree with everything Debbie said, because that might inflame her. She would say something positive. "Come to think of it, I cannot bear the thought of leaving my family. They are so helpless. I really want to help them rather than run away from them."

Hugging and leaning on Wendy, Debbie sobbed into her windbreaker. "I'm so ashamed. I want to help my parents too, but what can I do?"

Wendy soothed her friend as best she could. Suddenly, she brightened. "As soon as the restaurant opens, I'll speak to my father, and he'll let you come to help serve. You'll make some money then." Wendy patted her friend. "You always sound so positive that I never suspected any problems in your family."

"Thanks. But we are only fourteen, and I don't think your parents can hire me."

"Oh, yeah, the labor laws."

"I really wish my parents were wealthy, so I can be the cultured lady Mother wants me to be. As it is, maybe I should do some ironing sometimes."

"Would you rather play the piano?"

"Not particularly! But I think my sister is seriously interested in music, so Father had better not sell the piano!" Debbie wiped her face. "You gave me an idea! Perhaps I can get a part-time job in some Chinatown restaurant and ask them to pay me under the table!"

"I can ask Dad to pay you cash."

"Thanks. It'd be fun to work with you. In the meantime, I'll just have to do some ironing." Debbie kicked the wall again, still looking forlorn. But she was leaning back and not in any more danger of banging her head.

The wind did not let up, and the discussion depressed them. They decided to go home. With heavy, droopy eyelids, Debbie thanked Wendy and apologized again and again for being such a sad sack. Before letting her go, Wendy held her friend's face in her palms and kissed her forehead. Then she gave her an extra-long embrace and extracted another promise that she would not run away. Debbie kept her hands in her pockets. She leaned lightly on Wendy and mumbled her promise. She was afraid that if she returned the embrace, she might start crying anew. Somehow, it was so much harder to tell Wendy in person that in spite of the problems the House of Wong was having, she envied their escape from Chinatown.

A week passed. Wendy had hoped to meet David again at the orchestra rehearsals but did not see him. He seemed to have dropped out of orchestra altogether. When she caught sight of him at a distance, she hesitated to approach him. She was convinced that she would never talk to him again.

Coming home late one afternoon, she spotted him standing first in line, waiting to be interviewed by her parents in the back room downstairs. The Wongs were hiring a delivery and bus boy for the restaurant. This had been the first recommendation from Judge Bernstein: They must hire some neighborhood people instead of using only waiters from Chinatown.

Wendy strode right over, feeling so much more confident on her home turf. "Hey, what are you doing here? I was the new girl at the audition. Remember?"

"How could I forget? You were great! By the way, congratulations — I knew you would win." David extended his hand.

"Thanks." Wendy shook his hand. Her face flushed.

"You were awesome! Your flute made the music sound magical. It reached down and touched me . . . from the inside."

"I didn't have a chance to hear you play. I'm sorry you didn't win."

"Oh, that's okay." David laughed. Tilting his head toward the back room, he continued, "Now I have time to take on a part-time job. I can use the money. Are you interviewing for the job, too?"

Before Wendy could answer, David knocked on his head. "Oops! Can't be. They want a delivery and bus boy."

"No." Wendy laughed too. "I live upstairs. My parents and grandparents are the owners of this restaurant."

"Amazing! My parents own the DiVario Deli around the corner. I would work for them, but my older cousins took all the jobs there already. We live upstairs, too."

Wendy noticed a young man coming out of the back room. "Hey, now it's your turn. Well, good luck!" She raised her hand to wave but put it on her lips instead. She thought her heart would jump out of her mouth.

"Thanks!" He winked, waved goodbye, and headed toward the door.

"Grandma, Grandpa! I won the audition! I won both solos!" Wendy called out as soon as she entered the family quarters. Her voice rose much louder than she expected. Somehow, her brief conversation with David had left her energized and excited.

"That's really good, Wai Weh." Grandma took a sip of her green tea.

"Then we must all come to hear you," said Grandpa with a smile, smoothing down his wispy beard.

"You've inherited your father's musical talents, Wai Weh." The soft folds around Grandma's eyes gave her a permanent squint. She beamed with pride — winning a competition against the foreign devils was very exciting indeed. Her granddaughter must have inherited the proper genes from her family. "Your father never had lessons, but he could always reproduce any tune he heard on his harmonica."

"I know. He is amazing," Wendy joined in. "Last summer he practiced the Fourth Brandenburg Concerto with me. He does it all by ear."

"Your father has no time to play music now." Grandpa sighed. "Since that Stop Work Order, he's had to attend meeting after meeting after meeting."

Everyone fell silent. Wendy picked up her books to go to her room.

"Hello, everyone!" Mr. Wong greeted them as he entered the room.

"How was school today?" Her mother followed, addressing Wendy.

"School stinks," answered Winston, coming in last. He tossed his lunch box on the table and ran to the refrigerator to get a drink.

Grandma motioned everyone to "come, sit." She poured tea.

"We have good news." Mr. Wong grinned, uncertain of how his parents might interpret this kindness from the neighbors. "Mrs. Horton and Judge Bernstein have started a legal defense fund for us."

"Does that mean we can continue work on the restaurant?" Grandpa asked, wrapping his hands around his teacup as if in prayer.

"Yes, soon, I hope." Her mother frowned. "We have been asked to give certain concessions."

"What kind of concessions?" Grandma asked, jabbing an anxious finger in the air.

"I have agreed to a plain facade that will conform to the character of the avenue," Mr. Wong replied, looking into his teacup and avoiding everyone's gaze.

"We will have to forgo the red beams, golden dragons, and gold lettering for the House of Wong," her mother added with an air of gravity.

"What do the foreign devils know about the Chinese, to tell us what to do?" Grandma sputtered, rending the air with her hand.

"But why do they object?" Wendy asked.

"They don't want any 'gaudy display' of signs or advertisements," Mr. Wong explained. He straightened his shoulders and stood tall to lend dignity to his helplessness.

"I suppose then I won't be allowed to post my calligraphy of our daily specials on the door," said Grandpa, beginning to pace the floor.

"That's a shame!" Grandma scowled. "Your daily specials are written in the most sophisticated rhymes."

"They are really poetry written in the finest calligraphy," Wendy's mother added.

"The foreign devils are ingrates." Grandpa coughed to emphasize his indignation. "My grandfather came to America to build the cross-continental railroad. He was a genuine pioneer." He fingered his wispy beard and paused.

Wendy thought he might remind them for the thousandth time how his grandfather had been killed during an accident in the Sierra Nevadas working with dynamite. He might again ask: "Do you know how the term 'A Chinaman's chance' came about?" Then he would describe how the railroad builders used to place a Chinaman in a basket and lower him into a mountain shaft to ignite the dynamite. What were the chances of the Chinaman coming back out alive? Grandfather always sounded indignant, no matter how many times he told the story. Wendy could not imagine things like that had ever happened in America. After all, America had abolished slavery! Yet, deep down, she knew that these events must have occurred, because everyone understood the phrase "a Chinaman's chance."

"No one would talk about how my grandfather died, but his son, my father, was given citizenship. Yes." Grandpa coughed again to lend gravity to his thought. "And now they won't even let me post my calligraphy in my own restaurant!"

"We have also agreed not to set off firecrackers for our grand opening," her mother whispered.

"That stinks!" Winston cried. "I can't believe they won't even let us celebrate with fire crackers!"

"It is a fire hazard," Wendy's father explained limply. He gave his mother a pleading look. "We must be grateful to those neighbors who have already given us so much assistance."

Grandma's eyes twinkled with understanding. She stretched out her arms, moving them slowly and deliberately from side to side. She soothed him: "Ah-yah, so we give in a little here, a little there. The important thing is: Our restaurant will open!"

"Yes, that's the spirit!" Wendy's father shouted, slamming down his fist on the table a little too vigorously.

Grandpa sighed with resignation and paced to the other side of the room to stare out the window. Winston edged closer to his grandfather, leaning his head into his waist. Grandpa grasped his shoulder and remained quiet.

Wendy's mother finally whispered, her voice almost breaking. "They think we should be more American. They don't understand that it is hard to let go of old customs, because we were not given citizenship and allowed time to learn the language. We were always treated like aliens."

"Is it not also because you think it is more expensive to eat American food and do things the American way?" Wendy couldn't help the sarcastic tinge in her voice.

"Yes! But it is not just that the Americans charge more money. Since we never had insurance of any kind, we had to go to the Chinatown Chinese doctors, buy insurance from other local Chinese, and deal with bankers and others who speak our language and understand our old customs. Mrs. Horton is the first foreigner who has extended a hand to us."

Everyone nodded again in agreement.

"Sorry," Wendy mumbled. Somehow, in spite of the solemnity lingering in the air, Wendy felt relieved. Perhaps her parents had logical reasons to be stuck in the old ways. They were rational people, after all, and she must help them.

Suddenly, she remembered David DiVario. "Mom and Dad, did you finish interviewing the guys downstairs?" she asked expectantly.

"Yes," said Mr. Wong, happy to change the subject. "All the boys seem competent. Unfortunately, I can't fire all my old help from Chinatown, nor can I afford to hire more than one boy."

"We will hire more help when our business expands," her mother finished. "I'm sure our neighbors will understand. I can't say I liked all the boys down there."

"Oh, you mean the young men," Wendy corrected her. It seemed that ever since they moved uptown, she was always explaining the modern and "politically correct" things to say. "Since they are old enough to work, they'll feel insulted if you called them boys!"

"Oh, what's the difference?" Her mother brushed a speck of dust off her sleeve. "That Gary with the long, brown hair will make people wonder about his dandruff when he clears dishes. And that other one, with his spiked hair and black leather jacket, looks positively menacing. Who'd want to open the door to him when he makes a delivery?"

"C'mon, Mom. Lots of guys these days look like that."

"Well, that fellow Steve looks clean-cut and seems very enthusiastic. He knows the neighborhood well. On the other hand, David DiVario's parents own an Italian deli right around the corner."

"David is an honor student," Wendy announced quickly. She knew she was playing an ace for David, which set her heart racing again. "I noticed his name on the Honor Roll board outside the principal's office. And he must be a scholarship student as well if he has to find work after school."

"Ah, it would give the House of Wong plenty of face to have a scholar working for us!" Grandma exclaimed.

Grandpa turned around with Winston, and was grinning broadly now. The adults all looked as if they had been chosen for the Honor Roll. Scholars had always held the most prestigious position in Chinese society. Although they needed only a delivery and bus boy, Wendy knew she had tipped the scales in David's favor by mentioning his academic achievements.

"You have brought good fortune to the family, Wendy." Her mother looked at her with soft, warm eyes. "Mrs. Horton suggested that I sign up for more English lessons at the popular New School. She offered to substitute as the receptionist at the restaurant when I am in school." The New School for Social Research was a well-known Manhattan institution of higher learning. It catered to adults from various backgrounds who wanted to enhance their education.

"That's great, Mom!" Wendy and Winston almost cried out together.

"You may be able to talk properly to my teachers for a change," Winston added.

"Did you hear that Wendy won the audition for both solos with her orchestra?" Grandpa asked.

"I always knew my children would succeed," said Wendy's father, beaming with pride.

"Ah-yah, everyone owes her fortune to her life spirit or fate," said Grandma, jabbing a bony finger in the air. "You all know that Wai Weh was born in the Year of the Tiger. The time was one o'clock in the morning, which was most propitious. It is then that the ruling life forces of a tiger would be the strongest." She paused for breath. The atmosphere of the family council excited her, even though she had told the story a thousand times. She wiped her sweating forehead. "You also know she was named for Glory, so her honor must have been preordained," she concluded.

Wendy groaned. Her Chinese name sounded so strange in English! Few Americans could pronounce it accurately. "Oh, Grandma, it is only the school orchestra," she protested, and turned crimson.

Still, from her grandmother's point of view, she had been born to bring the family glory. Like most Chinese from a good family, her name had not been acquired casually. In fact, it indicated her genealogical position in the family tree. "Wong," the family name, meant "Emperor." "Wai," the generational name (which she shared with Winston), meant "to realize." Finally, her personal name, "Weh," meant "glory," "flair," or simply "élan."

"Ah." Grandpa cleared his throat. "Let us burn some incense in front of my grandfather's tablet. He was the patriarch who wrote this chastening poem for our family motto." Without a pause, he began to recite:

Inkstick glides on Inkstone round and round;
Serenity imbues the mind.
Fingers caress the brush.
Attack, pause, swivel, swirl,
Lightening and pressing,
The spirit is revealed.
Listen well!
Rise to Virtue!
Reaching ancient vitality:
The Harmony of Character and Home.

Everyone in the room was familiar with the poem. Each generation had taken a word from it to form the same second word of their generational name. Hearing her grandfather talk, Wendy would conjure up eerie visions of the Wong family as generations of ghosts gathered, forming themselves into a poem on parade.

"Ah, yes." Grandpa held his teacup with both hands, lifting it as if performing a ceremony. "The spirits of our ancestors will be smiling on you when the restaurant opens and you perform with your orchestra."

"Whoopee!" hollered Winston, who never missed a chance to tease. Hooting and skipping around the room, he sang, "The ghosts of our ancestors will help Wendy play her flute. Toot, toot, toot!" He puckered his lips and flapped his arms to impersonate flying spirits.

"Oh, skip it, Winston." Wendy widened her long thin eyes, pouting. "That isn't funny. We all helped." Unable to conceal her shy smile, she stammered, "I had better go and practice."

"Yes, stop it, Winston!" Grandpa grabbed the boy and addressed him by his American name. "A son of the family does not make fun of his ancestors."

All the adults nodded.

In the quiet of her room, Wendy began her usual routine before practicing. She set up her metronome and her music stand, and then sat down to clean her flute. The familiar motions calmed her, and she thought about the true reasons for the family's change of fortune. Indeed, having two railroad coolies and two cooks on the family roster was not the kind of pedigree most Americans would boast about. But then, the Chinese venerated their ancestors and lived with ghosts. Living in America, among so many "foreign ghosts," it was no wonder they called on ancestral aid with such frequency. Wendy grimaced at the thought of giving thanks to her invisible ancestors. Yet she was comforted by the sense of connection to the past where there was a home base that emphasized refinement, gentility, and harmony. The circumstances of the old might not have been easy, but she felt proud to be part of people who worked hard and were creative in dealing with challenges of life. Yes, the family's fortunes were changing, and a sympathetic scholar, a "real American," one David DiVario, would be working in their restaurant.

Debbie would never believe that my grandparents' prayers to the ancestors helped, Wendy reflected. *But she might agree that cooperation among the family in thoughtful discussion could probably help get them through any crisis.* Perhaps Debbie's ancestors would find a way to intervene in Debbie's family situation. In spite of her skepticism, she prayed to Debbie's ancestors.

~Chapter 6~

WENDY STARED AT the screen and made a sweet-and-sour face. She was just a tad upset that Debbie had not responded with much enthusiasm about her winning the competition.

I knew you'd win — you always do, Dee Sharp said.

So how are your parents?

Quiet. Mom insists that I practice my piano as usual and let her do the ironing. Dad is sullen, but accepting it.

Cool, your mother really loves you! Maybe things will chill.

Silently she thanked Debbie's ancestors. Maybe her prayers had helped.

Wendy observed that when two people fight, one must give in, or the relationship will break. In her family, the grandparents seemed to have adopted a policy of gentle persuasion. No one ever raised a voice. Her parents argued, but one of them would give in and move on. Wendy now realized how lucky she was to be part of this household. She hoped things would cool down in Debbie's home. She was so happy that there was no more talk of running away.

:(, :(, :(. Listen up! Dee Sharp wrote, *everyone is on edge because the DNA test confirmed the Chins' worst fears — the piece of flesh really does belong to their little boy!*

Oh my God, what are they going to do? Kween Be felt helpless.

Mom says the cops are useless. What's the use of calling them?

Grandma would say the cops wouldn't help because they don't care about the Chinese, Kween Be offered.

Not the point. They've still got to do something, right?

Right. So it's still good to call the cops. You never know.

Yeah, Dee Sharp agreed. *Ms. Chang, our new social studies teacher, said we should be patient and give the police a chance to do their work.*

Talk to you tomorrow. Maybe they'll get lucky. Love, Kween Be, signing off.

Wendy felt calm and reassured that Debbie was getting support from Ms. Chang, and sounded as if she was more concerned about Eddy's case now than about her family problems.

Through Wendy's persuasion, and after many discussions, the House of Wong asked Mrs. Horton to become a consultant on their renovations. The family wanted to be sure that the restaurant's new design would be in keeping with the neighborhood's aesthetic standards. Wendy was delighted. She had made it her business to keep Mrs. Horton informed about all the family's plans.

"Red is a lucky color for the Chinese," explained Wendy while visiting Mrs. Horton in her bookstore. "My grandparents thought up these elaborate plans — to use dim lights and this lucky color all over."

Mrs. Horton pondered the information and immediately agreed with Wendy that they must persuade the family to make changes. She drew Wendy's mother aside the next day and explained delicately that Westerners think dim red lights convey the impression of a house of ill repute, where prostitutes do business.

"Oh, no!" Wendy's mother exclaimed. She alerted the rest of the family, who abandoned their plan without protest. Grandma promptly offered more incense before the ancestor tablets to thank the spirits for delivering them from this terrible mistake. Mrs. Horton became a frequent dinner guest.

During one of the dinners, Mrs. Horton suggested that since the family was familiar with Western music, perhaps they could pipe in classical music instead of the Chinese tunes that were often uncomfortable for Western ears. Wendy offered to choose the music, and eventually everyone thought

Haydn, Mozart, Vivaldi, and other composers that they had heard Wendy practice were excellent choices.

The family stubbornly refused to make other changes in the decor. Since Wong meant "Emperor," and the dragon was the traditional symbol for the imperial throne, the adults were determined to have yellow dragons breathing fire from all corners of the dining room. Wendy's father also ordered a front door of red lacquer, with swirling golden dragons projecting regal opulence. Mrs. Horton did not have the heart to inform them that the neighbors might consider this design gaudy.

Seeking a tactful solution, she conferred with Wendy, and learned that the grandparents were avid gardeners. The next time she came to the Wongs' house for dinner, she brought a whole stack of books on Oriental garden designs. She told the Wongs that the Metropolitan Museum of Art's Astor Court is an exact copy of a famous Chinese garden in Soochow, China. In fact, it had been constructed by Chinese artisans sent over by the Chinese government. The family agreed to visit the museum to inspect the famous Chinese garden.

"But looftop galden we have." Grandma spoke directly to Mrs. Horton for the first time. She proudly led Mrs. Horton to their rooftop greenhouse, and showed her Grandpa's pride and joy. The array of bamboo, miniature orange trees, orchids, impatiens, hibiscus, geraniums, and endless varieties of flowering cacti was so impressive that Mrs. Horton exclaimed: "Why, you must display your flowering plants in your restaurant!"

Everyone was most amenable to the suggestion, so the interior design of the restaurant underwent a transformation. Although the front door was still tilted toward the south, the entrance now appeared to be an ancient temple gate. The Vermont marble posts and beams lent an impression of strength and dignity to the outdoor foyer. The foyer led to the circular rosewood front door, which was elaborately carved with swirling dragons. By now, the family had come to see red and gold as a poor match for the simplicity and natural beauty of a Chinese garden.

Inside, the reception desk and bar in the front of the restaurant were built like tea pavilions. Plants at the peak of their bloom enlivened the restaurant dining rooms, which featured an authentic Chinese garden theme. Tables were grouped on small terraces, surrounding a real waterfall and reflecting pool in the back. Tiled footpaths wound among the tables. The whole family was pleased with the new arrangement.

Everyone helped to choose the scenic scrolls and fancy calligraphy for the walls. The lucky red color adorned only the menu covers, on which "House of Wong" was embossed in gold. The appropriate golden dragonhead, projecting fire in relief, was also on the cover. The restaurant was ready to open for business before Memorial Day.

On opening day the Wongs prepared a huge twelve-course banquet for all the neighbors who had helped them with their legal defense fund. Judge Bernstein and his wife, Ambassador Ben Zvi and his wife, Mr. and Mrs. DiVario, and Mrs. Horton were all invited to sit at the head table with Wendy's parents and grandparents. Wendy's mother sat next to Mrs. Horton. Although Wendy's father excused himself between courses to supervise the cooks in the kitchen, he toasted and thanked the guests at the beginning and toward the end of the dinner.

Winston joined Debbie, Wendy, and David to form an efficient team clearing used dishes and supplying fresh ones for each new course. Throughout the dinner, Wendy watched and listened to every word and movement of the distinguished guests. They seemed thoroughly relaxed and happy to share a genuine Chinese banquet with the Wongs. Even though they all said this was a novel experience for them, Wendy could not imagine them ever feeling uncomfortable or ill at ease in any strange surroundings.

She observed that Ambassador Ben Zvi was short, with a pear-shaped build. He asked for seconds of steamed fish in wine sauce. He talked very little and had a soft, gentle way when he was spoken to. Mrs. Ben Zvi was slender and diminutive. Her alert blue eyes and short, curly dark hair gave her an impish look. She was not having much success trying to engage Wendy's grandparents in conversation. Judge Bernstein, with a head full of white hair, was tall and robust looking. His booming voice made everyone take notice when he praised the food. He was most fond of the crispy orange beef. His wife was stout, had well-coifed brown hair, and wore glasses. She also seemed very quiet. David's parents favored seafood in bird's nest but had trouble using chopsticks. In the end, Wendy had to bring them forks and knives. Mrs. Horton loved the Peking duck. David was a quick study while learning to insert a morsel of duck dipped in hoisin sauce, a piece of scallion, and a sliver of cucumber into a Chinese pancake. When Wendy complimented him, he replied, "Piece of cake! It's just like wrapping up a soft wheat taco!"

Winston served an individual small plate of Peking duck to each guest in the manner he was taught. Grandfather smiled and patted his head as Winston served him.

Wendy presented her friend Debbie to all the guests. Debbie had let her raven-blue bangs grow long and had her short hair cut forward at a slant. When she lowered her head, her tresses covered half her face. She blushed when introduced and allowed her straight hair to cascade forward. Someone mentioned the kidnapping of Eddy Chin. Debbie looked miserable when people lamented that the police hadn't found the boy.

"It is really good that the news media have become involved," Judge Bernstein said. "The publicity could save Eddy's life, because now the Snake Head gang know they'll get the death penalty if Eddy is killed!"

Debbie pushed her hair back behind her ears and flashed Wendy a triumphant smile. Wendy stared at Debbie, again wondering if she had been the one who had called the TV station. David noticed the looks and whispered to Wendy, "Is Debbie involved somehow?"

"We'll talk later," Wendy replied secretively. She took some dirty dishes into the kitchen.

Mrs. Horton sipped her wine while everyone discussed his or her heritage and cultural background. The Ben Zvis were Israelis. The Bernsteins had emigrated as children from Hungary and were raised in Brooklyn. "Leaving the ghetto is a quintessential American experience," asserted the judge.

"We grew up in Little Italy, right next to Chinatown," Mrs. DiVario contributed. Mr. and Mrs. DiVario were teenagers when their families came from Naples, Italy. "We went into many Chinese shops, but we never came to know any Chinese people until our acquaintance with the Wongs."

Mrs. Horton exclaimed to Wendy, David, and Winston: "We're the only native New Yorkers here!"

Everyone chuckled.

"With respect, but why you all so helpful?" Looking at Mrs. Horton, Wendy's mother finally blurted out the question that had also been weighing on Wendy's mind.

"It is true that my ancestors have been here for many, many generations," Mrs. Horton responded after some hesitation. "I have never really experienced prejudice and persecution." She raked her fingers through her curly gray hair. "Many years ago, I went to see the Broadway musical *Cabaret*. It was about the prelude to the Holocaust in Germany before World War II. People were throwing stones at Jewish shop windows; I was both moved and terrified. It was a hot and humid day, and everyone was wearing short-sleeved clothes. During intermission, I noticed many tear-stained faces. Some of these people had concentration camp numbers tattooed on their arms. Their suffering had been more horrible and vivid than what was enacted on the stage. Shortly after that, I met the Bernsteins and the Ben Zvis."

Grandfather stiffened when stone throwing was mentioned.

Mrs. Bernstein spoke for the first time. "Oh, that must have been more than twenty years ago. I remember that you told us your husband died just after World War II. You showed me letters he'd written you about the hideous conditions he saw while liberating the Nazi concentration camps for Jewish prisoners."

"Yes," replied Mrs. Horton in a small voice. "We were only teenagers. But my husband was sent to fight in Europe right after we married. So, in a way, I too have some understanding of how hatred of other races or religions can cause suffering. The stone thrown at your window reminded me of that horror and renewed my sense of outrage."

Again, Grandfather shuddered.

"We emigrated from the ghettos of Poland to Israel," Mrs. Ben Zvi whispered. "We know the horrors of being persecuted for our religious beliefs, or just for having been born Jewish, period. Hitler first used anti-Semitism to rally people against Jews so that they could not earn a living; only later did he resort to extermination as the so-called Final Solution to his 'Jewish problem.' We swore that this would never happen again — to anyone!"

"What is anti-Semitism?" Grandmother asked Wendy in Chinese. Although Grandma could understand some English, her vocabulary was limited.

Wendy translated. "I think that is when people don't like you just because you're Jewish."

"I hear that Jews are really smart, and always help each other out," Debbie chimed in. Wendy thought Debbie sounded bold. She knew her family would consider her forward and might not want to include her in their future parties. She wondered how David felt about prejudice and other matters of race.

"It is true that most people prefer to work within their own communities and interact with their own kind. We are certainly not unique in seeking to help each other in this way," Ambassador Ben Zvi answered.

His wife added, "People who belong to the same country clubs, church groups, political parties, often help each other out in times of need. We all like to conduct business based upon connections."

"Yes, such connections are very important in China, too," Wendy's father agreed. "But everyone helping us here is not Chinese." He raised his wineglass for another toast and thanked them all heartily.

Grandfather must have taken this discussion to heart. He was now sighing and apologizing in Chinese: "The Snake Heads don't behave like the Chinese. I'm ashamed of them — they kidnap their own kind!" Wendy's father translated.

"But Grandpa, you are an American." Wendy could not help interrupting. Grandpa's face beamed.

Wendy made a mental note to talk with Debbie about stereotypes at another time. She had always admired Debbie's spunkiness, but now she felt Debbie was being too forward and didn't know how to alert her. She hoped that her family could learn from the Jewish experience. She realized she was serving truly remarkable people. Mrs. Ben Zvi's simple remarks on the Holocaust made her want to hug her. Imagine, Mrs. Horton's husband had died trying to help others. Indeed, these were heroic souls!

"Did you see the headline in the *New York Times* a few weeks ago?" Debbie asked everyone, wide-eyed and pushing her hair back. "The Academy of Sciences published a report about immigration being good for the U.S. economy. It even said that most immigrants do not take away jobs from Americans."

"Shut up, Debbie," Winston whispered as he passed her. Both Wendy and David smiled at his wisdom.

"Yes," Judge Bernstein answered Debbie. "It is wonderful to get some scientific facts on immigration," he said in his booming baritone. "The Academy of Sciences speaks with authority, as it is a nonprofit organization of distinguished scholars."

Mrs. Bernstein smiled and nodded: "We are a nation built by immigrants. So many of us have endured hardship in a distant land."

"Yes, like the Vietnamese boat people's passage. They made daring escapes to come here. And they work so hard!" Mr. DiVario spoke for the first time. He and David seemed to have the same lines etched around their mouths.

"I just heard on TV the other night that half the people working in California's Silicon Valley are immigrants," Mrs. DiVario added. "America is gathering all the smart people in the world to create all these new important products — computer this and computer that!" She smiled, pointing from side to side with her fork to emphasize her point. Her animated gestures gave her words emphasis.

Looking at all the youngsters, Mrs. Horton raised her hands, giving two thumbs up: "Yes, it is the gumption and resourcefulness of immigrants that have made our nation so vibrant!" Somehow, the playfulness in her voice dispelled the solemn atmosphere.

"I have always enjoyed the international flair of this city." Ambassador Ben Zvi laughed. "Where else outside of Asia can you find such an authentic Chinese banquet?" To restore the festive mood, he once more toasted and thanked the Wongs.

When the steamed thousand-layer cake was served, Mr. Wong returned from the kitchen to toast and thank the guests, and invited the youngsters to join everyone.

"What do you want to be when you grow up?" Mrs. Horton asked Wendy.

"Oh, I don't know," Wendy answered slowly. She thought about her new uptown school where she felt more like a spectator. The Caucasian girls who fit in so easily with the scene would surely find their way in the larger society, but how would she? Looking at Mrs. Ben Zvi, she felt a burst of sudden inspiration. "One thing I do know — I'll help make sure that what happened to the Ben Zvis will never happen here!"

Wendy's parents had spoken only a few sentences throughout dinner, but now her father was nodding his head in agreement. "Many layers," he said, holding up the thousand-layer cake, "one sweet flavor!" His eyes sparkled, and he was grinning from ear to ear.

~Chapter 7~

THIS IS NUMBER-ONE girlfriend calling Kween Be:

Did you see the TV tonight? Eddy's safe! And they caught the kidnappers!

That's great, Dee Sharp! Was Eddy hurt?

He's fine. But it's pathetic to see how he clings to his mother and tries to cover his left ear by leaning his head against her.

Sick. What that child must have gone through!

Mrs. Chin says that she'll let his hair grow long, and soon he'll forget his mutilated ear. <BTW> I learned that now "sick" is the same as "cool."

Too much on my mind now, Kween Be answered. I'll stick to the old meaning. This teen talk can be a drag.

OK. Sick means sick! Anyway, they say kids change a lot. Maybe that also means Eddie will heal fast. Dee Sharp quickly reverted to Eddie.

Hope that's true. <AFK>(Away from keyboard)

Wendy stepped away from the keyboard to get a drink. She mixed up a cup of her favorite soft drink, Orange Tang. This was a private joke that always made her chuckle to herself. Oscar Tang in their Chinatown school told everyone he had a crush on Wendy. Wendy was not interested and said that her love was already taken by another Tang.

Debbie's message was on the screen when she returned.

<BTW> How about that Number-One Love Interest? That David is awesomely cute! Have you guys gone out together yet? Have you at least gone to a movie or something?

No, we've never gone out. We're just beginning to work together in the restaurant. Plus, we're seldom alone. I still dream of a heart-to-heart talk with him; someday soon, I hope.

He seems quiet, Kween Be.

Well, I don't know. <BTW> When we were serving the banquet, he wanted to know if you were somehow "involved" with the Chins.

Nobody's involved in the way you mean. When you live in Chinatown, you just can't help being part of local events. Wendy, you are so lucky to be working with David. Promise me you'll tell me everything about him!

I'll try.

Also, I loved the banquet! You can't find many conversations like that around here.

Yeah, those guests were special. I've never talked to people like that either.

<IMO> (In my opinion) I disgraced myself. I felt like a jerk afterward, like I was overstimulated or something. I sounded like a dork

from Chinatown. *That brother of yours is really smart. If he hadn't warned me, I might have said that all Jews and Chinese are smart; the immigrants do all the work; and the Chinese have the highest culture in the world! etc. etc. Jeez, why couldn't I just shut up?*

Wendy loved Debbie's capacity for self-examination. She was learning a lot from her. She quickly replied:

Relax, girlfriend. You didn't do any damage.

Thanks, but what I wouldn't give to trade places with you!

You don't have to. Come and help us serve anytime you want. Dad'll pay you the going rate when he can. We can always use an extra pair of hands.

Wendy smiled at the screen.

I'd better wait till your Dad asks me. I really was a doofus buying into all those stereotypes — and blurting them out, too.

We all do at times, Dee Sharp. Just think about it.

Yeah, Kween Be. It's easier to put people in a box and not bother to find out what they're really about. I think it's 'cause we're lazy. I mean, how many people want to trouble themselves with the details?

But you're not one of those Chinatown "group think" jerks, Dee Sharp!

Wendy couldn't resist asking her the question that had been on her mind for so long.

Are you the one who called the TV station about Eddy's kidnapping?

Yes, I admit it. Ms. Chang encouraged me, and this took my mind completely off my parents' problems.

Really? Cool.

Yeah, Kween Bee. Ms. Chang said if the Chinese remain isolated, we'll never be part of the melting pot. People will always think of us as sneaky, hardworking robots. She said we must have courage and show individual initiative.

Wow, you sure did!

Well, I don't know, but at least now they've caught the kidnappers.

Yes. Little Eddy lost an earlobe, but not his life.

Plus, in the future, would-be criminals may think twice about intimidating new immigrants.

You said it.

<BTW> Do you know Eddy's mother now teaches Chinese in a private school? The TV station supplied a lawyer to look into the Chins' immigration status. They might even qualify for political asylum because Mr. Chin was a democracy advocate in China!

Rocking awesome, Dee Sharp! You really did good!

Ms. Chang said, if you're open, innovative, and law-abiding, anyone can succeed in America!

Well, you certainly did your part.

You did good yourself, connecting your family with those wonderful people, Kweeny Be!

You too! How are your parents, really?

They seem fine. Dad bought my sister and me an old hourglass to put on the piano so we don't have to break to look at the time. It's a bronze and glass contraption and really looks cool on the piano.

Could be a piece of antique! Talk to you tomorrow, Sweet Sauce.

Wendy was glad that she did not have to confront Debbie about her behavior during the banquet. Somehow she felt that Debbie was American before she arrived. Perhaps, having longed for democracy and the rule of law under colonial Hong Kong, she had already received a fair helping of American vitality because of her faith in the American dream. Wendy's family, however, viewed Debbie as too brash. When people in Chinatown told them Debbie had called the TV station, they warned Wendy that her friend was too bold, and therefore not trustworthy. They would never invite her to help serve again. Wendy stomped her foot and started to protest, but her parents and grandparents gave her a big lecture on the paramount virtue of preserving "harmony" in the community. Since the Chins were illegal immigrants, Debbie had taken a big risk getting them into the headlines. Also, the Chinatown community was worried about getting a bad name. Any bad publicity would turn away the tourists and depress business, sowing seeds of discord. Wendy wanted to argue, but she wasn't comfortable doing so. She had never been a rebellious child. Her home was her sanctuary, and she shared the struggles of the family, especially since they moved uptown. Wendy was not sure how to best defend her friend.

Straddling the world of an American school and a Chinese home, Wendy felt her alienation from both. Though the restaurant was now in full swing, and the community's support promised to make it a thriving business, the family remained insulated from neighborhood affairs. No one had been arrested for throwing that stone, and the family was still apprehensive. Because of the surging flow of customers, and Officer Hogan's frequent presence (often standing in front of the alley to listen to Wendy's flute), Wendy never heard any more drug dealing in her alley.

Some days her mother would invite Officer Hogan in for a cup of tea or lunch, but this was rare. Except for an occasional visit from Mrs. Horton, the family never socialized with anyone outside the front door.

Busy with the redesign and grand opening of the restaurant, Wendy's mother had missed the registration date for her English classes at the New School. Wendy was disappointed. However, her mother didn't seem too concerned and was happily occupied with the thriving restaurant. Secretly, Wendy had hoped to see her family become more truly integrated into their new community. She was convinced that language would bridge the two cultures and put much hope in her mother's English classes.

Everyone still spoke only Chinese at home. Wendy cherished the rhythmic cadence in her grandfather's recitations of Chinese poetry, though she had never studied Chinese literature.

In her new school, she was learning to love the music of English poetry as well. "I bet Mrs. Horton would understand alliteration," she mumbled to herself as she entered the restaurant one day. "Alliteration," she recited, "a poetic device wherein words in a line begin with the same letter in order to enhance its sonority and rhythm." She remembered a verse of Lord Byron:

She walks in beauty, like the night
Of cloudless climes and starry skies.

"Or like my name, Wendy Wong Wai Weh, or my friend David DiVario!"

Wendy mused: *Oh, wouldn't it be wonderful if my home culture and my life in school were the same?* Perhaps she could encourage her grandparents to befriend Mrs. Horton. Her father needed to go to Chinatown every day to shop for fresh produce, but if the rest of the family could satisfy their social needs up-town, then perhaps she could tell her school friends that her parents had named her Wai Weh Wong on account of their love for poetry. Of course, that would not be completely honest. Her parents did love Chinese poetry, but they would not know what the word *alliteration* meant. They had never gone to American schools. Her grandparents faced a huge language barrier, but there was still hope for her mother.

That night, Wendy tried to coach her mother to sound more cultured: "When you meet Mrs. Horton, ask her if she liked the sound of my Chinese name. It has the effect of being 'onomatopoetic.'"

Her mother looked puzzled.

"That is a poetic device for using words that sound like their meaning," continued Wendy, "such as buzzing bee, winnowing wind, and Wai Weh the wind player!" Wendy laughed, pleased with her invention. Her mother frowned.

"What do you mean by 'another-poe-tic'?" Her mother pronounced all "strange" English words in her peculiar Chinese way. "Poe means mother-in-law in Chinese," she said. "Am I crazy to want another mother-in-law?" She laughed.

"Oh, Mom!" Wendy cried in frustration. She clasped her head between her hands. After more than thirty years of living in America, Mrs. Wong still heard Chinese when she came across new English vocabulary. What could Wendy do but give up?

When Wendy was done with her homework the following afternoon, she went downstairs to help. David had just come in for work, and everyone began assembling the complimentary packages that went with all the takeout orders. Each small wax-paper envelope was packed with two Chinese tea bags and two fortune cookies. Wendy enjoyed these mindless chores because everyone talked and joked as they worked. Today, it appeared that her mother was still thinking of the fascinating new word Wendy had introduced.

"David," she said smiling, "do you know why we call Wendy Wai Weh, or the way you Americans call it, Way Way?"

"No, ma'am," David replied.

"Because it's another poetic. That means another mother-in-law in Chinese." She began to laugh. "But in English, it means Way Way the wind player."

David smiled politely, but his brown eyes widened.

Wendy blushed. "Mother is teasing me," she explained. "Did you ever come across the word *onomatopoetic* in English lit?"

"Quite awesome." David laughed as he began to understand Mrs. Wong's joke. "Another poetic, now that's cool. Does it really mean 'another mother-in-law' in Chinese?"

"Sure." Mrs. Wong chuckled. "Maybe that's why you're named David DiVario the Deliverer!"

David lifted his bushy dark brows and broke into a raucous laugh. "Double cool! That's a good one."

Wendy joined in. She was secretly pleased that her mother had understood the meaning of the word, even if she could not pronounce it properly.

The front door swung open with a loud bang. Everyone looked toward the entrance. A fat man with a dark mustache swaggered in. He was followed by a mousy-looking little man with a receding hairline.

Everyone stared. It was only 4:30 in the afternoon. The lunch trade was over, and dinner was at least an hour away. Wendy's mother ran over quickly to greet them. "Good afternoon . . . We . . . not ready for dinner yet!"

"Just get us two beers!" the fat man answered gruffly as he pushed the little man into a chair. He did not join his friend, but sauntered toward the door that led into the family quarters.

"Please, sir!" Wendy's voice was shrill. She reached the door before the big man. "That door leads to our private quarters!" She had forgotten to lock the door after she came downstairs. Now she stood blocking it and pointed toward the restrooms: "The washrooms are over there."

The big man tried the fire exit door instead. It, too, was locked.

"I go get you gentlemen two beers!" Mrs. Wong was too scared to send the interlopers to a nearby bar. The two men looked decidedly unfriendly. She ran into the kitchen to get her husband.

"Why is this door locked?" The fat one asked, shaking it.

"Sir, are you the fire inspector?" Mr. Wong rushed in from the kitchen, wiping his hands on his apron. Wendy's mother quietly served the beers.

The two men wore casual sport jackets and blue jeans. Were they the same two she saw lurking in the alley before the restaurant opened? Now that Officer Hogan was often around, Wendy seldom met people loitering or panhandling outside anymore. And these two certainly looked like gangsters. Or — she remembered reading about such types in newspapers — they were here to demand extortion money!

The robust man ignored Mr. Wong's question and gave them all a disdainful glare. "Are there any other exit doors here?"

"The fire exits are unlocked when the dinner trade begins," Mrs. Wong answered anxiously.

"Make sure they are!" The big man smoothed his mustache with his forefinger and walked into the men's room.

"We cannot offer you a menu because the kitchen is not ready to serve anything yet," Mr. Wong said to the mousy man sipping his beer. He had donned his frozen smile.

"Hmph. You speeky good English!" The little man snickered. "You cooky good Chink food, too?"

"Velly good food," said Mr. Wong, bowing. His face betrayed no emotion, and Wendy grimaced to hear him slip into the pidgin lingo expected of him.

The big man came out of the bathroom after a short while. He marched over to his companion, threw down a ten-dollar bill, and said to the little man: "Let's go!" Turning to Mr. Wong, he continued in a more conciliatory tone. "Better luck next time! Come back chow-chow soon."

"Yes, yes . . . velly good luck next time! I guallantee! Evellyone happy, eat my place." Mr. Wong was grinning with relief. "Yes, thank you for coming. Goodbye."

"Good grief, Dad, why do you have to talk like that?" Wendy asked when the men were gone. She knew the answer all too well. She was asking for the benefit of David, who looked puzzled.

"Obviously, the men were inspectors looking for some sort of violation. I speak the way I'm expected to so I won't offend. I certainly don't want to appear superior." He ran into the men's room to check.

He shrugged when he returned. "I can't understand that fellow. He opened the small vent window leading to the alley. Otherwise, he didn't touch anything!"

"Drugs. That's it!" Wendy shrilled. "Remember the time I overheard some guys in the alley when I was practicing?" She did not mention the family plan to catch drug dealers. That would have been too much to explain to David. "I can't remember exactly, but they mentioned getting money to knock someone off and buy snow — something like that. Do you think they're connected?"

"Why would they come in here?" David asked.

"We had better seal that window," Mr. Wong said. "The man probably wants to make sure he won't be observed when he makes his deals in the alley. It is best not to offend the drug dealers!"

"Is that why you speak pidgin, to please them?" Wendy asked, disgusted. "Oh — " She covered her mouth with one hand and gave David a guilty, sidelong glance. She remembered she had been instructed never to show any disrespect to her family in front of a foreign ghost. And in any case, wasn't she supposed to keep quiet about her eavesdropping advantage from her room? Well, David did not seem to have noticed.

"We have to make a living," her father said simply. He looked at David. "These people could have been some hostile neighbors!"

David hesitated before lifting his eyes from the floor. "I have never seen those guys around, Mr. Wong. I wonder what they want." He shook his head.

"We only ask to live and let live. Giving in verbally is a small price to pay for peace." Mr. Wong turned toward the kitchen. "Get on with your work."

"Americans . . . so strange; ways we not understand," her mother added when they resumed their work. "They also think our food more genuine when we speak funny! It sure make trouble learning right English."

David replied: "My parents are first-generation Americans, so naturally they have difficulties with the language. Wendy once told me that she is a fifth-generation American." He could not understand the Wongs' troubles, given that they had been in America for so long.

"I am the first generation born and educated in this country!" Wendy answered for her mother.

"Grandfather's grandfather died helping to build railroad, so his son, Grandfather's father, was given citizenship." Mrs. Wong's fingers flew while packing the fortune cookies. "When railroad finished, he work for some rancher and became cook.

All the while, lots of trouble for all the Chinese here. Many, many Chinese, to escape persecution and massacre, went back to China."

"I didn't know there were persecutions and massacres of the Chinese in America!" David gasped.

"Oh, yes, there were! There was the Chinese Exclusion Act," Wendy blurted out. "When the American economy was in recession, the Chinese, who worked hard for less money, were seen as a threat. Racism had become so common that a law was passed to exclude them. I mean, uh . . . us!" Wendy turned red, uncertain as to how she should identify herself. She lowered her head and felt both ashamed and confused.

"I think I remember reading about it." David's eyes bulged in astonishment. "While America welcomed European im-migrants at Ellis Island, the Chinese were kept like prison-ers for months and years on Angel Island in California. The poems of their suffering were carved on prison walls — I even believe some have been published. I know American history has not been untainted by racism, but I always thought it had more to do with relations between blacks and whites."

"No, racism was practiced against the Asians and Native Americans, too," Wendy whispered.

"True, but we fought a civil war over just these matters, which makes it doubly hard to identify with that part of our history." David's hand reached out toward Wendy, but he stopped short of touching her when he glanced at Mrs. Wong.

"In times of mass hysteria, people can forget to be human." Wendy's voice trembled. She had noticed David's gently outstretched hand and felt his sympathy.

"Because Chinese could not naturalize like white people, the government not care about protecting Chinese people from raiders or bullies." Tears welled up in Mrs. Wong's eyes, but she turned her head and blinked them away. Straightening in her chair, she continued. "Since the Chinese Exclusion Act did not allow the men to bring their families here, Wendy's grandfather was born and raised in China even though his father was already an American citizen. But war is always happening in China, so Wendy's grandfather also came to America and became a fabulous cook." She sounded cheerful now. "So Wendy's father was born and raised in China as well until he was old enough to come here as a son of an American. You see, they were always — how do you say it?" She said the word in Chinese to Wendy.

"Sojourners," Wendy translated.

"They made sure we speak bad English, only pidgin."

"When did you and Mr. Wong come to America?" David asked.

"Mr. Wong in the early sixties." Mrs. Wong smiled, and so did her wing-like eyes. "I left Shamchun in the late sixties with Wendy's grandparents. They, American citizens, retired in Shamchun." She finished the rest of her thought in Chinese and let Wendy translate: "The political situation in China at the time — China had the Great Cultural Revolution — was too dangerous for them."

"They brought my young mother here to marry my father," Wendy said with a wicked grin, breathing a sigh of relief. She was glad to lighten up the conversation because she always felt a pain in the pit of her stomach whenever they talked about their traumatic family history.

Her mother blushed noticeably. "Wai Weh, I'm not slave girl — *mui tsai*. I was not a wife by mail order! Your father and I distant cousins. I was cashier in the restaurant on Canal Street more than three years before we get married."

"I really like the way you fixed up the restaurant," David said with a smile. His hands were busy, but his curly brown head gestured toward the greenery surrounding the dining room. "My mother called this the classiest restaurant on the East Side."

"That is Mother and Mrs. Horton's contribution." Wendy smiled with obvious pride. Her eyes resembled flying wings, like her mother's. "Mother never finished high school in Shamchun, but next fall, she will be attending English classes at the New School." Wendy paused. David was staring at her intently.

Both Wendy and her mother blushed. David averted his eyes and changed the subject. "I am always fascinated when you do your work on the abacus, Mrs. Wong. Your fingers go flying clickety-clack, and next thing you know, you tell us the cash register is incorrect. And you're always right!"

"I don't trust computers!" Mrs. Wong exclaimed. "New electronic machines very good, but my abacus never short of gas." She waved her hand with her thumb in the air.

They all laughed.

Placing the last wax-paper package into the box, her mother told Wendy, "I think you'd better go upstairs and finish your homework now. Grandpa and Grandma will soon want dinner. David, set up ten tables for four here. Then come in kitchen and have your dinner."

Although there was still a feeling of nameless unease and many questions lingered in her mind, Wendy was accustomed to hearing news of violence and other strange, outrageous acts occurring in New York. Smiling and relaxed, she ran up the back stairs to her room. In the company of David and her mother, Eddy's kidnapping and her own experiences with the rock throwing seemed less real and threatening. She still could not fathom the meaning of all that was happening. At any rate, her home life was sweet.

She loved her mother's sense of humor. She would have loved to tell Debbie her mother's joke about "another mother-in-law," but it just didn't seem right to brag about how much fun she was having with David around. If Debbie asked, she would say that David was adjusting to the family's strange ways, even though he was often puzzled.

Wendy could not tell her parents about Debbie's family problems, but she complained to them about not inviting Debbie to help serve at their restaurant, just because she had called the TV station.

The family had overcome the neighbors' antagonism. Now business was booming. Grandma and Grandpa both remarked that the Wong fortune seemed to be turning. For her part, Wendy had never had so much fun helping in the restaurant. Her thoughts wandered to the spring concert, and she looked forward to practicing. For the time being, she forgot about those two overbearing, horrible men.

~Chapter 8~

THE NEXT DAY, David stopped Wendy in the school hallway. He slapped her a high five.

"Hey there, Miss Wong, going my way?" He grinned. "Your dad wants me to work extra today, but I have a physics exam coming. Can you help me clean up the 'garden' area? Please . . . I'll bring you some of my mother's lasagna!"

"Cool." Wendy smiled. "That's a fair exchange." Wendy loved Mrs. DiVario's food.

"All right! Thanks, Wai Weh." David imitated the Wong family's way of pronouncing her name.

Wendy didn't mind David's familiarity. She certainly preferred working with David to that of another *fokay*.

When David and Wendy came down the restaurant's garden path that afternoon, Winston was scrambling up and down the tables and chairs, watering and pruning the plants in the room.

"What a mess!" David sighed.

"Stop climbing on the tables, Winston. You're going to fall and crack your head!"

"Don't scream at me, Wai Weh," objected Winston, hopping from one table to another. "I'm only doing it because Grandpa told me to." Grandpa was the family's self-appointed authority on plants.

"I'm sure Grandpa wouldn't want you to break your neck!"

"I won't!" shouted Winston. He pinched the plants here and there, muttering "listen, Wai Kuo," imitating his grandfather by changing all the *r* and *n* sounds to *l,* and using long *e* sounds for short *i*'s. "Lumber won meestake is watel too much. Lumber two is glowing wild. Juss like keeds, callot let glow wild!" Winston fingered his imaginary beard now and then, and lowered his voice as he croaked his lecture standing on the table.

David and Wendy doubled up with laughter. "Nice going, Winston. Fantastic impersonation," David said.

"Listen, Wai Weh!" Winston picked up a tulip-shaped wineglass, clutching it in his hand as if it were a microphone. He shook his head like a performer and let out a blood-curdling yell: "Ssssspeshow, special, House of Wong!"

He pointed to David and Wendy:

What you want?
Dragon and Phoenix,

Sesame Sticks.
Shrimp and Chicken,
All orders taken.
Study your menu,
Enjoy your view.
Blown lice, white lice, flied lice,
All fair plice!

He stepped and hopped from table to table, swinging his hips.

Try some ginger squid,
With a fat spare rib.
Never pause,
Ssspechull sauce . . .
Say, yo, want some wine?
Blow your mind . . . To peeeg heaven!

He gave them a wink, spun around on the table, raised up his "mike," kicked out one foot, and yelled, "What! Can I take your order please?"

David stood gaping at Winston. "I don't believe this! He's doing rap!"

"Seriously, what a ham." Although Wendy disapproved, she was clapping.

"Sssspechull! House of Wong!" Winston returned to Grandpa's voice, but still rapping, stepping, and swinging: "You born Ahmelican, you born lonely. You born Chilese, you born beeg . . . beeg family. Spechull, sssspechull. Velly good luck."

"Winston, that is enough!" Wendy said, dragging him down from the table. "David doesn't know what you're talking about anymore."

"Of course he does," said Winston. "This is rocking cool! Grandpa said when you're born an American, you are given a name all for yourself, but we Chinese get the whole family."

David and Wendy moved two tables together.

"What Winston is trying to say, David, is that according to Chinese custom, your family name comes first, your generational name comes second, and then your personal name follows as a part of it all." She gave the table a vigorous wipe and decided not to mention the family poem, her vision of her ancestors' spirits on parade, or how she had been named to bring the family glory. "For instance, my name is Wong Wai Weh, and Winston is Wong Wai Kuo. We both share the first two words; only the last word is our own."

Winston stuck his face right under David's nose. "Grandpa said that if I ever go to China, I'll know someone is my cousin if his name begins with Wong Wai something."

"Hmm . . . Sounds cool, but I still don't totally understand." David frowned into Winston's eyes. "How come you are also called Winston and Wendy?"

"I'm named after Winston Churchill, 'cause when I grow up, I'm going to smoke a big cigar and become a great leader!" Winston marched around, sticking out his stomach, and puffing on an imaginary cigar formed by extending his thumb and little finger. "Wendy's lucky she wasn't named Wanda the Witch by that registrar in school."

"Huh? Really?" David asked. The House of Wong was always full of surprises. "Are you pulling my leg?"

Wendy blushed. "Oh, Winston! Stop teasing." She made a face. "You're getting fresh!" She pushed Winston through the door and locked him out. "We'll never get anything done with that clown around."

"Seriously, did the registrar in school name you Wendy?" David asked, shaking out a tablecloth.

Wendy grimaced. How was she to tell David that a registrar in school named her?

"Umm . . . You know how many Americans can't pronounce Chinese names." All her blood seemed to have surged into her face. She paused to collect herself, and turned away to spread out fresh table linen. "Most Americans call me Way Way, but you know the Chinese call me Wai Weh. The first word has a downward inflection, and the second an upward one." She took a breath and had to slow down. "Well, when I was ready for kindergarten, the woman couldn't pronounce my name even after my mother had repeated it several times over. Finally, Mom suggested that the registrar choose a more American name. That's how I was named Wendy. To this day, I have no idea who that woman was."

David continued setting the tables and looked away from Wendy while he absorbed the information. On his next trip to the service pavilion where all the glasses and silverware were kept, he brought out his package.

"Why don't you eat the lasagna now before it is completely cold?" He tore open the paper bag, turning it into a place mat. On it he set down the container of lasagna, a glass of water, a fork, and a napkin. He took Wendy's hand and stroked it with his thumb, as if he had done this a hundred times before, then he drew her over to the table. Gently he pushed her into the seat.

Wendy felt her hands burning, but she only smiled. "Wow, I'm so hungry I could eat a horse! Thanks. Want to get a plate and have some too?"

"No, thanks," David replied. "I'm saving my appetite for your father's awesome food later." They laughed. Wendy was happy David had changed the subject and that she did not have to keep explaining Chinese ways.

As David watched Wendy eat, he reached for her free hand again and stroked it with his thumb. A bolt of lightning ripped up Wendy's arm; she wondered if smoke might be pouring out of her smoldering body.

"When I was a kid, I used to worry about the way my parents talked, too. Now I'm used to it. I think it's okay," David shared.

Wendy knew she was flushed all over, but she did not withdraw her hand. "I know sometimes I put my parents, especially my mother, on the spot to show that she is educated in spite of her poor English. Of course, I can accept my parents speaking with an accent. But sometime they, like, exaggerate and talk pidgin just to pacify some bully!"

"That stone thrown at the restaurant and the Stop Work Order must have really scared them," replied David after some thought. "But now the customers keep coming."

"My parents would do anything for the restaurant." She laid down her fork. Her appetite had left her.

"Maybe that's why they're so successful," David said reassuringly as his thumb continued stroking her palm.

"But when are they ever going to stand up for their rights instead of letting such creeps walk all over them? Sick, real sick, isn't it?" She worked desperately to concentrate on the conversation.

"I'm not so sure. I bet your father could take care of them, if they pushed him too hard. He is awesome, seriously!" David winked at Wendy and finally let go of her hand. "Eat. It'll get cold!"

"When your family only associates with other Chinese, people tend to think you're part of this secret, shadowy group. So dorky. Don't you think that encourages all the prejudice against Chinese Americans?" Wendy hovered over her food, picking at it.

"But how can they help themselves?"

"They can try, can't they?" Wendy was not so forgiving.

"You know, sometimes I think we come down too hard on our own parents. It's too easy to start thinking like everyone else." David leaned close. Wendy did not move out of the way. She let herself look more deeply into his eyes, comforted by their sincerity.

"Yeah, but my family can't seem to get out of Chinatown in their heads!"

"People all over the world behave just like they do, until they learn to communicate with each other. I read this story a while ago that really brings home how most people behave." David picked up a fork and started pecking at Wendy's food. He motioned her to join him. "There was this peddler who went from village to village in Poland, selling needles, buttons, and stuff like that. He was always giving things to all the children and young mothers who needed village things."

"Like thread or ribbons?"

"Yeah, maybe. Anyway, he was a Jew, and everyone assumed he was a smart businessman. They said he had secret connections to other successful Jewish people. They said he was rich and so it was okay to accept things from him.

"One year, the winter was very harsh, and people didn't see the peddler at all. 'Oh, he must be taking it easy in some chateau or rich friend's house,' they said. When spring came, they were surprised to find the peddler dead in his wagon. He had died alone, of cold and starvation."

Wendy was moved. "Oh, God, so like a Chinese," she said with a sigh. "The poor man would not beg because he wanted to save face!"

"Well, maybe, but you know, the villagers assumed he was rich and smart just because he was a Jew! You see? That's where anti-Semitism and thinking in stereotypes can lead."

"And they all took advantage of him! Plain sick," Wendy chimed in, finally eating the lasagna.

"Seriously. They thought or imagined that just because he was a Jew, he belonged to a big secret community that was good in trade. They probably also assumed that all Jews were involved in shady smuggling!"

"Just like they assume the Chinese are hardworking and sneaky." Wendy looked up, her eyes wide with recognition.

"Exactly. I can't tell you how many times I've been teased about my family's supposed ties to the Mafia!"

"Oh, my God, I never thought about that."

"Yeah, when you're not on your guard, everyone seems to slip into group think."

"You're right. I mean, here we are in a minority, yet my parents and grandparents carry these stereotypical ideas of other racial groups too. They still call others 'foreign devils, Japs,' and other such names. How did you handle it when people assumed you were part of the Mafia?"

"I used to get upset, but then I decided to tell them Robert DeNiro is my cousin."

"Awesome! I mean, like, really?"

"Well, at least as real as Leaky Boots' being your uncle."

Wendy started to laugh. "Nice move! But let's face it — there's no way you can make your family change their habits. I mean, think about it."

"Seriously, no one can change another person's behavior."

"Come to think of it, you're right. I guess we'll just have to take things with a grain of salt!"

"Maybe, but people like Debbie, Winston, you, and I will break out of the stereotyping. And that could be amazing."

Wendy smiled. "Debbie, especially. And you too!"

"You know," David said with a nod, "in spite of my mother's Italian accent, she is right about how this country attracts the best talents in the world."

"Oh, yes, you always hear that America is the financial and technological leader of the world! It's awesome seeing so many foreign faces involved in these . . ." Remembering her own face, Wendy stopped short.

David seemed to have guessed her thought. "Wendy, you don't have a foreign face — not to me anyway!" He was smiling at her, and his eyes danced with laughter.

Wendy lowered her head, her heart thumping furiously. She put down her fork.

"By the way." David continued to pick at the food. "Your parents came over especially to invite my family to the spring concert in school. I bet they're real proud of you. We're all looking forward to it."

The image of her grandparents, parents, and her little brother filing into the auditorium flashed before her. The vision of her grandmother's attention-getting finger pointing her out, "There is my granddaughter!" made her heart thump louder. She twisted her hands together. Sometimes, such a supportive family was definitely a burden. It was simply a part of being Chinese that they all felt obliged to share in her accomplishments. Winston was right: "When you born Chilese, you born beeg family." Every member helped bring success to the family, so they all shared in its glory. This concept was just too complicated to explain to David.

Instead she said, "I . . . I'd better go and practice now."

"Way Way — do you think we could go see a movie sometime?" David leaned close and grabbed both of her hands.

"I . . . I . . . I . . ." Wendy was blushing so furiously, she couldn't say a word.

"Say yes." David peered into her eyes. He was near enough to kiss her.

Wendy could feel his nose tip brushing against her cheek. Her face felt suddenly large and pulsing, and the sound of David's breathing seemed a melody whose notes were whispering secrets. She shivered and pulled away reluctantly. Years of inhibition and strict family injunctions against early romantic entanglements called her back into her body. Before moving uptown, the grown-ups in the family had lectured Wendy and Winston that in a mostly white community, they would become informal ambassadors of the Chinese people. The family would demand model behavior from the children, especially in their restaurant.

Wendy's muscles tightened as she straightened herself. Her mother had told her any number of times that "foreign" boys were only interested in using Chinese girls for sexual experience. These thoughts brought on a cold sweat. She shook her head. "No, not just yet."

"Oh." He looked to the ground.

Wendy wanted to throw herself into his arms and get lost in the fantasy of a love affair, but Wai Weh, with an effort, restrained herself.

"Someone may come in here any minute. I've never gone on a date, and I must ask my parents' permission."

"Really? Never?" David stared. "Perhaps on a double date with another couple?"

"Never alone or with another couple."

David shook his head. He couldn't believe there was an attractive freshman in high school who had never dated.

"You know my family and my work schedule."

"Well, I know your family is different."

"You mean by different that we're Chinese, don't you?"

"Yeah, Chinese, but more like a nice old-fashioned family."

"I wish they could be more like everyone else."

"Will you be able to date when you go away to college?"

"I don't know." Wendy lowered her head. "Right now, I'm only worried about keeping my grades up for a college scholarship and scraping together enough money to pay for the expenses." She almost let it slip that she was a scholarship student and wanted to ask whether David was also on scholarship. Somehow, although she had never asked, she felt certain they were both in the same situation.

"I'm saving for college, too," David replied. "But that doesn't stop me from going to a movie once in a while."

"I'm sure Mother would give me permission if I asked. Actually, I think everyone in my family likes you and would allow me to go. I just feel awkward about asking." She made a face. She knew she was telling a half-truth. The family did like David, but they probably would not let her go to a movie with him — not alone anyway. They might suggest that Winston go with them. Imagine having Winston baby-sit her! Then, there would be all the questions after the event. It was not worth the effort.

"You know, it sort of surprises me that a modern girl like you still needs permission just to go see a movie!" David said.

"I guess I'm not that modern." Wendy lowered her head again. "Do you think I'm dorky or something?"

"Oh, yeah, definitely dorky!" David laughed. "But a beautiful dork!" His thumb was stroking her hand again.

Suddenly, like a morning tide that spreads over and warms the surf, a strange surge swept over Wendy. She felt grateful for David's sensitivity, and that gratitude came out all at once in a rush. She stood up and pulled him from the table. She leaned close, jumped on her toes, and gave David a warm peck on his cheek. "David, you're awesome. It's always super-fun working with you!" She ran upstairs.

Now it was David who blushed.

~Chapter 9~

WENDY FELT HOT and thirsty. She went into the kitchen, fetched a glass of cold water, and rushed into her room, telling her grandparents she needed to start practicing.

She closed the door and window, her heart still beating wildly. She was so agitated that she knew she might spill out everything if she e-mailed Debbie. She needed some time to mull over the experience. This had been her very first heart-to-heart talk with any young man, and she savored the strange tingling warmth and dull ache inside her. She still did not know how to handle the pulsing sensation that made her insides murmur. Somehow, Wendy felt that David had made her transparent. She had always taken for granted the total embrace of her family and used it as a shield against the larger world and her internal stirrings. Her aim had always been to study hard and to help her family prosper. Without realizing it, she had pushed aside the concerns of her maturing body and turned her head away from all the teenage romances going on around her. She had often mentioned to Debbie that these open liaisons were "yuckie." Debbie never contradicted her. They were like two voyeurs, still giggling and gossiping about other girls' adventures. Most of the time, they would either lambaste some girl for being "boy-crazy" or admit that so-and-so was "so cute." But their energies had always revolved around excellence in school and entering music competitions. Wendy had never even acknowledged to Debbie that she had found David attractive from the very beginning.

"Oh, why, why am I such a dork?" Wendy cried. Hot tears rolled down her cheeks, which she wiped away with the back of her hand. But David had called her a beautiful dork. She cried some more. "Why have I been born a Chinese American? Why can't my family be like everyone else's?" She sobbed and sobbed. "Why do I have to be an A student all the time? Why is the family always telling me that I represent not only the whole family, but all the Chinese? Who gave them the right to make me their ambassador?"

She remembered her mother telling her there was no equality in the world, how people were born with different endowments. She would have to make the best of what she had been given. She had come across the word *churlish* yesterday and liked the way she had to curl her lips to say it. Now she wondered if David might think her churlish, and if it wasn't her "Chinese pride" that was causing her to act so differently from other teenagers. Well, she was different: Her family dominated her, and her family had made her into a dork. But David seemed to think it was okay.

Wendy rose to get some tissues. She blew her nose and wiped her face. She felt so hot. She pulled off her sweatshirt and with an automatic motion took out her flute. Instead of playing, she skated the polished cold surface of the flute up her bare arms. When the flute slid by the inside of her wrist and the top of her hand, where David had held her, she trembled at the memory. The sensation was unfamiliar. Several times in the past she had wondered if she was attracted to some boy in school, but she had never felt such heat and thirst. She remembered the soft stroking of David's thumb on her palm. She raised the flute up to her cheeks and let the cool metal surface rub against her face, wondering how David's skin would feel with the stubble on his chin.

Was she falling in love? Was this what love felt like? Should she ask her mother? She knew what her mother's answer would be: *Just stay away. David will be going away to college in the fall. He will leave all high school attachments behind, and you're better off keeping him as a distant friend.* Should she consult Debbie? No, she'd better not write to Debbie just yet. Debbie might goad her into a deeper romantic entanglement. Then what would the consequences be? There was no way to keep things secret in her family. There would be an uproar and never-ending lectures from the grown-ups about bringing disgrace to the family and the whole Chinese population. And there would be endless teasing from Winston. She recoiled from the thought.

What was this tempest coursing through her? She told herself that she thought of David as a dear friend and coworker. But that wasn't all. She had been impressed by his kindness and attention the first time she met him at the school audition. She had always thought him really cute. Now she knew he could be tender, and realized that in her mind, he had become a dear, sensitive young man. And even, she felt, a little dangerous. She put on her sweatshirt again.

She decided to e-mail Debbie in the evening but not to mention any details. *Should I mention that he doesn't think I have a foreign face?* She wondered. *Maybe not. It's not important anyway.*

She turned toward her music stand and started practicing. After a half-hour, the metronome was still clicking and her foot still tapping. She was determined to do the triplets correctly. They had to be even, and she was increasing speed every day. *Now let me try it at 120.* She always worked up a sweat, so she stopped. She opened the window, touched her toes several times to stretch her muscles, and then resumed.

Now I am running all the notes together! This is too fast. I'd better go back to 112. As Wendy adjusted the speed, she heard voices with harsh accents coming from the alley.

"I've got more snow this time. Free sample."

"Thanks. Is the job here yet?"

"Yeah, it's here — in this joint."

"This is the loudmouth's favorite joint?"

"Yeah," answered the other gruff voice. "Eats here all the time or orders takeout."

They're talking about our restaurant! Wendy was suddenly alert. These men spoke with a foreign accent, definitely not Chinese. They were not the cooks and *fokays* from the restaurant. She would recognize those. Who were these strangers? People who sent the stone-thrower? Foreign drug dealers? Was a big-time drug deal going on down there? She hadn't heard anything for a long time. Plus, she had been doing repetitive exercises. Officer Hogan probably stayed only to listen to melodic tunes, so he was not going to be down there. The men seemed to be right beneath her window. Were these the same ones she had heard so long ago?

"So, the loudmouth ambassador loves Chinese food."

"Yeah, perfect place for a stomachache that can't be traced, if you get my drift." A guffaw.

"You're a smart planner."

"Yeah, can't point to us, for sure. That just leaves the restaurant!" Another full-throated laugh followed.

Wendy drew in a big breath to steady her nerves, playing on automatically while her thoughts still focused on the conversation below. *Are they talking about Ambassador Ben Zvi getting sick in the restaurant?* Her mind raced.

"Why don't we just hit him?"

"Maybe secret bodyguards watching . . . hard to hit 'im without getting caught!"

Are there bodyguards watching the ambassador?

"The boss checked out the place yesterday. Says there's no easy way out."

Oh, no, now he must be referring to those two awful intruders! Wendy began to panic. *That means the fat man is their boss! What should I do? I must tell Father. What about our plan for me to alert the family? The family will call Mr. Lee. Is there time for Mr. Lee to call the police if I start playing the national anthem now?*

"So whaddaya gonna do?"

"Something really clever! We're gonna let the great ambassador choke eating Chink!" He laughed repulsively. "On a little extra seasoning . . ."

"He'll eat it?"

"Comin' from this place he will!"

I wonder what that means. Maybe they're the two who said their boss was asked to knock off someone. Should I play the anthem now? Everyone is sure to be in the restaurant kitchen. Wendy wondered if her notes would travel as far as the restaurant or whether anyone even remembered their agreed-upon signal to call the cops, or Mr. Lee. She worried that no one had mentioned the alleyway for a long time.

"The fire exit doors, see, they have a special lock from the inside."

Wendy heard dull thumping on the metal doors followed by a soft tapping of fingers on wood. *They must be trying the fire exit door and the boarded-up window vent of the men's room. What do they want? They are not discussing drugs, so I can forget about playing the national anthem.*

"We'll have to move fast. They want 'im knocked off before he makes that speech next week. Here's another sample for ya."

"Ah, good."

"So you want in?"

"Mmmm, good quality. Sure I want in."

"Good. So you'll go rent the car?"

"Sure. You can tell your boss I'm clean. No one can trace me to you or the loudmouth."

"Yeah, you're not connected."

Wendy gasped. *They've already made all the plans! Surely that can only mean Ambassador Ben Zvi!* Wendy knew that the ambassador was due to make an important but controversial speech at the United Nations the following week. All the TV news stations were talking about it. Some other countries in the Middle East were not pleased with the attention it was receiving.

Ever since the House of Wong opened, the Israeli ambassador and his wife had favored the garden room. Several times a week they would either dine by the reflecting pool or order takeout.

I should really take a look and see who these people are, Wendy thought, playing on. *I'd better not stop my music, or they may get suspicious.* With her flute still in playing position, she edged closer to the window. Peering down, she saw two brown-haired men walking away, one wearing a blue parka and another in a dirty gray sweatshirt. She could not see their faces. When the alleyway looked deserted, she ran down into the kitchen.

"Dad, Dad! I have to talk to you." She was all out of breath.

"Wai Kuo teased you about your name again?" Her father smiled.

"No, no, no," Wendy gasped. "Come to the front room — right now! I have to speak to you in private." The cooks must not find out that from her room she could hear every word spoken in the alley.

"Oh, these teenagers are so impatient," Mr. Wong complained to the other cooks in Chinese as he slowly washed his hands.

"Please hurry, Dad! Please — it's important!"

Wiping his hands on his apron, Mr. Wong followed Wendy into the front room.

"Now, what's the matter, Wai Weh? You look as if you've seen a ghost!"

"Dad, they are going to kill Ambassador Ben Zvi!" Wendy's heart was pounding so hard that she could hardly breathe.

"What? Did the TV say that?"

"No, Dad. I was practicing with my window open, and I overheard two men talking in the alley. It wasn't about drugs, so I didn't play the national anthem." Wendy spoke rapidly, fingering an imaginary flute to help her father understand. Then she waved her arms toward the men's room and the fire exit. "They said their boss had already checked out the place yesterday! Remember the two weird guys who came poking around? These two, the ones in the alley, work for the Fat Man. And he sure wasn't a fire inspector!" Wendy sounded as if she was hyperventilating.

"What? What are you talking about?"

"Remember the two guys? The ambassador — they called him the loudmouth — they want to kill him!"

"Yes, of course I remember those two weirdoes. What makes you think they're killers?"

"I heard them tapping on the fire exit door and the window vent from the men's room."

"Are you sure they're not fire inspectors?"

"Oh, Dad, of course I'm sure. What are we going to do?"

"Your mother remembers them. We will watch out for them," her father assured her, still wiping his dry hands on the apron.

"C'mon, Dad, you must call the cops!"

"And tell them what? That you heard someone outside who wants to shoot someone called Loudmouth? No."

Wendy was getting even more agitated. "No — no shooting. Poison! They said they can't hit him without getting caught because of the bodyguards watching him in secret." Wendy stamped her foot for emphasis.

"You're not making any sense. I've never seen any bodyguards. You must have heard wrong!"

"No, no. I'm not telling you right. Just let me start over." She pressed her hand on her chest and took a deep breath. "Remember how, before the restaurant opened, I overheard two men talking about knocking off some politician?"

"Okay, but that never happened. And besides, what's that got to do with us?"

"Maybe it's going to happen now. And it's going to involve our restaurant!"

"Why should it?"

"They said he'll get a stomachache that can't be traced!"

"Nonsense, no one gets sick eating here." Her dad still missed the point.

"But their plan may be to poison the ambassador!"

"Oh, no. Not in the House of Wong they won't!" Her father glared at her.

"Even though they called him Loudmouth, I know it must be the ambassador. They said they were going to get paid to have him knocked off before he makes that speech to the United Nations next week!"

"Wendy, are you certain you heard all this? What did they say exactly?"

Wendy's speech slowed down a few miles an hour. "Dad, they said that we, the Chinks — that's what they called us" — she swallowed — "are going to help them 'put a little extra seasoning' in the food! That he's going to 'choke eating Chink'! Something like that. Oh, Dad, are you or aren't you going to tell Officer Hogan?"

"No, no, no, we're not going to help anybody that way! We're not going to get involved with the police or anyone like that." By the way he was bunching up his apron, Wendy knew he really meant what he said.

"Let me think about it first. Perhaps it was only a joke?" Mr. Wong was still fiddling with his apron. "Mr. Lee will be having dinner with us this evening. I will come up and discuss your . . . whatever you heard . . . then."

"C'mon, Dad. I told you what I heard!" Wendy stamped her foot again insistently. "Shouldn't we do something right away?" She almost shouted.

Wendy knew she did not have Debbie's immigrant gumption. The adults were the decision makers in her family. She could not pick up the phone and call the police herself. And anyway, who would believe her?

"Don't worry, Wai Weh," soothed her father. "The family will take care of everything."

"But you must call the police!" Wendy was frantic.

"It is always a big problem for a Chinese to get involved with the police. We are who we are," Mr. Wong replied, unruffled. "We don't want anyone throwing stones at our restaurant again." Mr. Wong clenched his fists, looking intently at Wendy. "Don't be rash and bring dishonor to our family. And make sure you don't mention this to anyone — especially your friend Debbie."

"But Debbie helped save Eddy's life!"

"Yes, but how is that our concern? We don't want her calling TV stations again, telling everyone our food is poisoned! Wai Weh, don't you dare talk to anyone outside this family! We just need time to think things through."

Wendy wanted to scream. Adults always needed so much time to think things through. She wrung her hands in frustration. "Surely the police and Ambassador Ben Zvi should be told. And soon!"

"Wai Weh, have you lost your senses? Am I supposed to call the ambassador and tell him there is poison in our food? You want the police or the Board of Health to shut us down on account of this?"

"Oh . . ." Wendy groaned.

"Now, remember! Not a word to anyone, not a soul!" Her father wagged his finger at her. He paused, softening his tone. "Anyway, your mother remembers those two characters. We'll decide what to do if they come into the restaurant again."

Wendy knew she should not e-mail Debbie; her father would be furious if Debbie called a TV station. He did not feel the same urgency, and the rest of the family would agree with him. Besides, he would not act without consulting his clan and its trusted adviser, Mr. Lee. Oh, why, why, why was her father so . . . so Chinese?

~*Chapter* 10~

WHEN MR. LEE arrived that evening, the gathered family consulted around the dinner table. Wendy's father told Mr. Lee and the entire family what Wendy had overheard from the alley.

"No, Wai Weh, you should never breathe a word of this to anyone!" Mr. Lee warned, looking sternly at Wendy. "You will have to close your doors for sure if anyone suspected poison was put in your food. That would be a great loss of face."

"But we have to tell Ambassador Ben Zvi!" Wendy cried. "You worry about losing face; he might lose his LIFE!"

"And you will lose your restaurant! Now, let me think." Mr. Lee ignored Wendy. "As I was saying, what you heard maybe only a joke or an empty threat. Besides, if you told the ambassador, it would keep him away from here. And then the people who want to poison him would never be caught."

"Let's tell Officer Hogan." Wendy was talking very fast again, but no one seemed to share her urgency. Her father did not even hear her. He responded only to Mr. Lee.

"That's right," Mr. Wong agreed, clasping his hands together for emphasis. "In fact, I can have full control over the ambassador's order so that nothing can happen to him here."

"That's true. You buy the food, you cook it, and you can trust all the other staff." Mr. Lee placed his work-roughened hand on Mr. Wong's shoulder, giving him the full weight of his confidence.

"Yes, I will tell the cooks to keep the side door locked, and I will turn up the air-conditioning so that no one need go into the alley to cool off." Her father gave everyone a reassuring glance. "In fact, I will serve them myself, or have my wife act as their waitress."

"Dad," Winston chimed in, "I can help watch out for the crooks, too!"

Wendy couldn't believe she was hearing this. Should she tell Debbie and David and ask them what to do?

With one elbow propped on the table, Wendy's mother rested her chin in her hand, thinking aloud. "We must do the right thing for everyone. It is our duty to safeguard the ambassador and our restaurant." Looking straight at Wendy, she continued: "We'll tell Officer Hogan, too. We'll just say we don't like to see so many panhandlers on our street. But not a word to your friends! Words have a way of spreading." She wagged a finger as she spoke. "Before long, everyone will be saying that our food is poisoned."

"C'mon, that's not telling the truth! That's not what it's all about!" Wendy gripped the edge of the table tightly to steady her nerves.

"We don't want the House of Wong to get a bad reputation," Grandma whispered, dabbing the sweat from her face with her silk handkerchief. Her quiet voice brought icy fear into Wendy's whole being.

"This might be nothing more than the empty talk of drug addicts. We don't want to see heavy objects flung through our window again!" Grandpa said with a raspy cough.

Wendy sighed. If only they could tell Officer Hogan the whole truth, he would surely protect the ambassador. "Shouldn't we at least ask Mrs. Horton to help us look out for her friend? The Ben Zvis are victims of the Holocaust, and we owe them so much!"

"Certainly not! We have bothered Mrs. Horton enough as it is," Mr. Lee replied. "Besides, Mrs. Horton and the Ben Zvis are close friends. She will feel duty bound to warn them. It is precisely because these good people have already suffered so much, and because we owe them the restaurant's survival, that we must do something by ourselves to protect them."

Everyone nodded, except Wendy. Somehow she did not feel reassured. *What would Debbie or David do? I really don't know because I can't even ask them! Do I lack the courage to disobey my parents? Am I just scared of taking on the responsibility? Am I being stupid? Surely the grown-ups know what they're doing!* She felt ashamed recalling her bravado when Mrs. Horton asked about her life's ambition during the restaurant's grand opening banquet: "I will make sure what happened to Mrs. Ben Zvi will never happen here!" she had blurted. Oh, what could she do? In the House of Wong she was still considered a child, and the role of a Chinese child was to listen to the teachings of the elders and obey. She knew better than to continue arguing.

Her father was already thinking ahead. "But what if the ambassador orders takeout food? How can we make sure he gets it safely?"

"Oh, you can trust David to deliver it safely," said Wendy, straightening her shoulders.

"Yes, I can trust David to deliver it, but what if he got wind of the threat? What if he talked?"

"He won't talk."

"If there should be the slightest rumor of anyone tainting our food, we might just as well close our doors, Wendy," her father intoned in earnest. "The reputation of this restaurant has taken my whole life to build!"

"You know, Wai Weh, there may still be some hostile neighbors out there!" Grandpa coughed again.

Wendy sighed from the depth of her being. She didn't know what to say. It would be hard not to confide in David and Debbie, but she could understand her father's fears. Until they had befriended Mrs. Horton, the Ben Zvis, and the Bernsteins, the Wongs had never trusted Caucasians and people not considered part of the family — especially after the Stop Work Order and the stone throwing.

Wendy reasoned: *Debbie might have helped Eddy. What can I do to help? We certainly cannot survive the publicity of someone trying to poison our food! Though David is a loyal employee, he is not family. Would it make a difference if he were my boyfriend? No, given my family's objections to any romantic entanglements, they may even fire him. Oh, but the survival of the restaurant is at stake! Except for an occasional day off, my parents have never taken a vacation. All they've ever cared about is the success of the House of Wong.*

Wendy realized that all her life, she, too, had been devoted to realizing their dream. Aside from her ambitions in school, perhaps it was her own dream as well.

"It is also our responsibility to help protect the family," Winston informed his sister in the most solemn voice Wendy had ever heard from him. "And I am willing to do my part."

"Yes, Wai Kuo, you are absolutely right," Mr. Lee agreed. "We are in this together. Everyone must help. There is no need to panic and cause anyone to think of the word 'poison' in regard to your food. After all, Wai Weh only heard some whispers. That is no guarantee of harm, except to your reputation."

"We must act in a normal fashion. Not a word of this must leak outside the family," Grandpa said fiercely, looking at his grandchildren. They understood.

"It would be a good idea if someone followed your delivery boy," Mr. Lee added. "Just in case —"

"Oh, oh! I'll tail him! I'll tail him!" Winston thrust himself forward, waving his hand as if he were answering a question in his classroom.

"Wendy, you can help here." Mrs. Wong did not accept Winston's offer but opened a palm toward Wendy. "Whenever a delivery call comes from the Ben Zvis, you'll have to follow David."

Wendy shuddered. *So, this is my part in the family intrigue. I must do the right thing. I must obey my parents, my grandparents, and the wise Mr. Lee. I must be brave and somehow protect the ambassador, too!* Wendy felt a chill creeping down her spine.

"Oh, let me, please let me tail David!" Winston pleaded. "Wai Weh is only a girl, and I'm brave!"

"No, no, no," Wendy's mother insisted. "You're too young!"

"Oh, dear." Wendy did not know what to say. Winston's agitated eyes bore down on her. Wendy foresaw a dare forming. Her jaw set in a firm twist, she nodded. *I have been given an important role,* she thought. *Winston would love to take my place, but he is definitely too young. Can I handle this responsibility, which involves the lives of such precious friends? I must do my job well! What if I saw David attacked? I must have a plan of action ready . . . to protect the ambassador, and myself.*

Mr. Wong seemed to have read her mind. "Don't worry, Wai Weh — trust us. The whole family is behind you one hundred percent!"

"Oh, yes, trust the family," she echoed. She knew this as the Chinese solution to everything. She felt overwhelmed by the united force of the family decision. *I need peace,* she thought. She slipped away from the family conference for the quiet of her room. She needed to be alone and to contemplate a plan of action.

She would make sure to stay vigilant and not be a coward. Without having to think about it, she knew that — as for most youngsters — the security of her family was the foundation of her life. She could not risk losing that. How could she go against the family that had worked so hard to establish itself in this land?

When Wendy chatted on-line with Debbie that evening, she mentioned how she and David had talked about stereo-typing people, but did not breathe a word about their near kiss or her family's plan to protect the ambassador.

~*Chapter* 11~

SPRING SHOWERS CAME the very next day, and so did a call from the Ben Zvis. They did not feel like walking to the restaurant in the rain, they said, so requested a takeout order.

Wendy's stomach churned and her hands shook as she put on her light parka to prepare to follow David. Winston was waiting by the front door — he had been ready long before her.

Wendy should have known that when her father said the whole family would be behind her, that meant Winston, too. A Chinese child was never shielded from the realities of life, especially when they involved the family. Of course, Winston was more than enthusiastic about the family's new intrigue to save Ambassador Ben Zvi.

"Where do you think you're going?" Wendy questioned her brother.

"Grandpa said I could follow you. If you need any help, I can run for it."

"Good grief, Winston! You're too young. I have no time to look after you too!"

"You always act like an American big sister! Grandpa said if we were in China, I'd be responsible for you because I am a boy."

"So what does sex have to do with it?"

"Sex has everything to do with it. I'm a boy, and I can run faster. Anyway, I am coming, and I'll take care of you."

If Wendy hadn't been so nervous, she would either have blushed at her own preoccupation or laughed at Winston's self-importance. "You know you mustn't talk about this ever, to anyone outside the family," she warned instead.

"I know. I'll be cool. You'll see!" Winston sounded serious but confident. He grabbed Wendy's hand.

"Okay, you and I will follow David from a distance; everyone will think we are just out for a walk." She trudged along. "Maybe it isn't such a bad idea to have you come along after all. At least no one can tease me that I'm mooning over David."

It turned out to be an uneventful trip. Wendy tried to be observant. She studied the passersby, their posture, the stiffness of their necks, the shoes they were wearing. Did they look familiar or treacherous under their raincoats and umbrellas? Did anyone look like the Fat Man, the Thin Mousy Man, or the two she had seen walking out of the alley? She could not decide. All that raingear certainly did not help.

When they returned, Winston looked dejected as he plodded into the kitchen to make his report. "Nothing happened, Dad."

"Winston was disappointed we didn't get into a game of cops and robbers." Wendy snickered.

"That's good," said her father. He was busy cooking. "Perhaps what you heard was only some kids fooling around?"

"Perhaps Wendy just heard wrong," Winston added.

"No, I heard right. I'm sure!" Wendy said, feeling a little hurt. "You don't have to come with me next time, Winston."

"It doesn't matter if Wai Kuo goes or not," said her father. "But Wai Weh, you should continue to follow David to make sure everything is safe."

"Okay." Wendy went upstairs. She felt relieved that she could resume her usual routine of doing homework and practicing flute.

The next day it rained again, and, right on schedule, the Ben Zvis called for a takeout order. This time Winston seemed too absorbed in watching *Star Trek* to be interested. Wendy put on her windbreaker and went out alone. When David left the restaurant, she followed, keeping a block's distance between them.

David quickly rounded the corner by the DiVario Deli. Wendy raced to the corner, but when she got there, he was nowhere in sight. She began to sweat. A mixture of adult and childish concerns swirled in her mind. *Should I go into the deli and ask if they have seen David? What excuse should I give? I can't have David's parents think he's goofing off from work. I certainly can't tell them why I'm tailing him. I'm sure they don't know David asked me out to a movie. Oh, what should I do, what should I do? Maybe he's been hurt! Did someone attack him? Kidnap him?* Her heart was pounding so hard, she felt short of breath. She spun around and dashed toward her restaurant for help. When David suddenly appeared, she stumbled as he accidentally tripped her with his folded umbrella.

"Oh, you're safe, you're safe! But you almost made me fall flat on my face! Why were you hiding?" Wendy was annoyed but relieved by the sight of him.

"Hey, Wendy, why were you stalking me?" This time David did not offer a high five. He was calm and very distant.

"Oh, I . . ." "You and your brother were following me yesterday, and you were doing a terrible job of it, too. When do you two ever go window-shopping together? Since when do you and your brother have an interest in antiques?" David stood beside Wendy but did not look at her. "Winston can't be interested in any of the shops around here, so why are you snooping on me?"

"Oh, David, I wasn't snooping on you. I mean, I . . . well, you'll just have to trust me!"

"The question is whether you trust me. Does your father want a report of my performance on duty?"

"No, no, David. It's nothing of the sort."

"Then what is it, Wendy?"

Wendy tugged at the zipper of her jacket, repeatedly running it up and down. She reddened and stammered: "I . . . I . . . I . . ." She could not continue.

"Okay, Wendy. If it is so important, you can walk with me to the Ben Zvis. I have to get this delivered, or everything will get cold. As it is, I can blame the delay on the rain. So let's walk and talk!"

Wendy trudged along miserably. The rain was coming down cold and biting, disguising the tears on her face. David had opened his umbrella, but he did not invite Wendy to share it. She knew that David would not forgive her deception, especially as she hadn't provided any explanation. What could she do? Any betrayal of family solidarity was unthinkable.

"I've got it!" David stopped short in his tracks. "It has something to do with the Ben Zvis, doesn't it? Both times you followed me, I was coming here to the Ben Zvis."

Wendy was startled by David's rapid deduction, but relieved to have an alibi. Grateful to have such an intelligent friend, she stepped under David's umbrella without saying a word.

"Awesome. So let's see . . . Mr. Ben Zvi has been in the news a lot lately. Could it have something to do with that new proposal he's supposed to present next week?"

Wendy nodded gravely.

"Cool," said David, obviously pleased with himself. Wendy smiled into his eyes. It was fun to play detective together.

"Well, what does that have to do with you and your family?" David lifted his eyebrows and stared at Wendy for confirmation. "I know this has to have something to do with your family because you're not talking, and you have no other reason to follow me."

Wendy gave an awkward smile.

"Yes." He nudged Wendy. He probably would have hugged her or given her one of his famous high fives if his hands had been free. "Your family told you to follow me when I took this food to — no! Is there something wrong with the food?" His face darkened. "No, no, that can't be."

Wendy nodded, her eyes blazing with admiration.

David was so busy trying to solve the mystery, and Wendy so intent on watching him, that neither noticed a big black limousine following them. It stopped silently. Four men in dark clothes jumped out, held guns to their backs, and shoved the two of them into the car.

Wendy tried to yell for help, but someone put a piece of tape over her mouth before she could make a sound. Pushed facedown into the floor space between the front and back seats of the limousine, with her hands and feet tied together behind her, she could only look on as David was given the same treatment. They now resembled two piglets trussed up for roasting.

~*Chapter* 12~

THE FAT MAN with the dark mustache sank down into the leather-backed seat with a sigh. "Let me have the bag!" he barked. *He is the same man who barged into our restaurant last week!* Wendy realized, wincing. She thought David also might have recognized him, the way his eyes were bulging.

The man sitting beside the driver handed him the bag from the House of Wong. "So, we meet again." The Fat Man gave David a little kick as he laughed. He opened the bag and took out the small wax-paper package of tea bags and fortune cookies. He tossed them aside.

"Ben Zvi's fortune is in my hands. He doesn't need these cookies."

He took out the first carton from the bag and opened it. It contained salmon fillets in a bird's nest. He picked up a piece of fish with his fingers and ate it.

"Um, not bad. These stupid Chinks sure know how to cook!"

"Boss, I always liked chop suey."

"This ain't no chop suey. Look, it's real pretty. Red peppers, green onions, pink salmon, and them black mushrooms all wrapped up in a golden basket!" The Fat Man was gulping everything down. He obviously would have enjoyed eating the whole carton by himself.

"You gonna put stuff in this?" The assistant licked his lips.

Was his one of the voices I heard? Wendy thought in desperation.

"Look, you can even eat the basket!" The Fat Man smacked his lips and shoved the assistant away, showing him the food. "Know what? This here made of deep-fried noodles. Hey, you, Chink girl! Did you cook this?" He gave Wendy a jab with his wing-tipped shoes, leering at her.

"Mmm, mmm, mmm . . ." Wendy made noises around the tape.

"Ah, ain't it too bad you can't talk. I must go eat at the House of Wong someday." He licked his fingers and began to wrap up the carton. "Hey! This won't pass. The poison might taste funny in this white sauce. We better not eat too much of this. Let's see what else we've got." He opened the next carton.

"Hah, this is it! Chicken and almonds in Szechuan sauce. The hot spices will cover everything. That loudmouth sure knows how to pick his food. I ain't never tasted chicken this tender!"

"Oh, the loudmouth sure knows how to" — the assistant swallowed — "how to talk too." He tried not to think about the food. "He has everyone in the UN under his spell."

"But not for long, my friend. The Chinks are going to help us take care of that. So simple! The loudmouth won't know what hit him." He was pleased at the thought. He winked at Wendy as he took out a switchblade and a vial. He flipped open the knife, waving it before Wendy's and David's faces. He made menacing motions and laughed again. David turned his head to avoid seeing the man's rabid face, and Wendy made more terror-stricken noises behind her tape. The Fat Man opened the vial, shook some white powder into the open carton, and carefully stirred it with his knife. Wendy wished that he would forget himself and lick the knife, but his colleague handed him a rag and he wiped the sticky blade thoroughly. Wendy froze, thinking that he might harass them again, but he snapped the knife shut. He returned the cartons to the paper bag and stopped the car.

"Hey, Joe," he called to the young man sitting next to the driver. "You take this to the Ben Zvis. Get a cab so you won't be too late, and say the usual delivery boy is goofing off with his girlfriend." He winked at David and kicked him again.

Joe left the car and slammed the door. They drove on.

Wendy felt sick to her stomach. David squirmed but could do nothing. There was nothing Wendy could do, either. She could not scream, and with her hands and feet tied together behind her, she could not kick. Even her threatening glances would not hurt a fly. She noticed the wax-paper package of tea bags and fortune cookies on the floor beside her. Perhaps the Ben Zvis would notice something was wrong when they missed the fortune cookies? She prayed and hoped. Her arms and legs were hurting, and her stomach on the floor of the car registered every bump on the road.

Oh, I failed! I failed! Wendy groaned miserably to herself. *Now the ambassador will be dead, and the House of Wong will be shut down forever! No one at home even knows we have been kidnapped. Oh, if only I had told Debbie! Surely she would have called the TV station by now, and someone would have been sent by helicopter or wailing police cars to rescue us.* The sleek limousine rolled on without a whine from the engine. It purred like a kitten. *In my nightmare, I could protect Eddie; now I can do nothing. Oh, no, I am not having a nightmare. This is a nightmare!*

The driver's voice interrupted her thoughts. "What should we do with these two?" *He sounds just like the guy who said he would rent the car!*

"Dump them into the river, of course," the Fat Man replied between laughs. He took out a cigar and began to smoke.

Soon the car was filled with fumes. Then he smiled and said, "Come to think of it, let's let the lovebirds live. We can drop them off at Juan's house." He laughed again. "By the time they're discovered, our mission will be over, and no one will find us."

Their lives might be spared, but Wendy wasn't thinking about her own life. Instead she plotted what to do to save Ambassador Ben Zvi and the House of Wong. She arched her back as far as she could, but her head was way below the window, and she could not get a view. The light droplets of rain that had splattered them now turned into a slapping curtain against the opaque window.

Laughing sourly and taking a big drag on his cigar, the Fat Man puffed the smoke straight into Wendy's and David's faces. They started choking. Their mouths were taped, and breathing was almost impossible. Their eyes teared up and their noses dripped. Wendy swallowed desperately, trying to catch her breath. Her face felt as though it were on fire. Her pulse roared in her ears. She was suffocating. She turned her head trying to avert her eyes from David's suffering. It was too painful to see him go through all this because of her and her family.

"Look boss," the gruff-looking man said, "they're crying for joy they don't have to die!"

"Hee-hee." The Fat Man giggled, jabbing David with his foot again. "Aren't you glad you won't have any more deliveries tonight? Too bad I can't let you free to fool around with your girlfriend!" There was more repulsive giggling.

Wendy closed her eyes. She could not stand to look at those lewd smiling faces. At least she could pray. To God? The family did not believe in one God. They prayed to all the gods in the Jade Emperor's court, and they invoked the help of the ancestors. How was she to do that? Grandma must already be burning incense, she thought.

Closing her eyes calmed her. *I took on this challenge, and I must be brave. I had better take a good look at these people so I can identify them later.* She opened her eyes. The smoke filled them. She blinked and stared, but her eyes were tearing so badly that the men's faces were a blur. She closed her eyes again and memorized their voices instead.

I must figure out the direction we are going. I must think of a way to get loose. Wendy swallowed hard. *We were walking south on Park Avenue when they got us. I remember we made two major left turns, so maybe we are still going north.*

She could hear the rain pounding steadily on the roof. The familiar sound was soothing, and she was filled with disbelief that she was awake. *Could this be happening to me? Are my sheets and blankets in bed suffocating me?* The pain from her tightly bound legs and wrists gave her a stab of reality. *Oh, my God, I am really living this horrible nightmare!*

"Tarxi, tarxi . . ." It was a Hispanic woman's voice. *We could be passing through Spanish Harlem,* Wendy thought, *or that could have been a Spanish-speaking woman hailing a cab in midtown. This is hopeless.*

She wished it weren't raining so hard. The street music of different Manhattan neighborhoods was distinct, and she should have had no trouble distinguishing which was which. The Asian sensations of Chinatown were familiar. The commercial sounds on Fifth Avenue, the clippety-clop of horse hooves around Central Park were surely different from the booming hip-hop music and laughter of children and street life in Harlem.

Now her chest on the floor was feeling the steady rumble of the car's wheels on metal. They must be crossing a bridge. They did not pay a toll, so it must be a small bridge. She was now almost certain they were passing into the Bronx.

Suddenly, the car stopped and the men roughly rolled her and David out. They grabbed them by the shoulders and dragged them into a building with the blue jeans of their knees and thighs scraping the dirty wet ground. Like two slain animals caught during a hunting trip, they were hauled into the elevator of what appeared to be a warehouse.

Though the two captives were terrified, the fresh air felt invigorating. Wendy kept her eyes open and caught a glimpse of the street. Everything around her appeared like a bombed-out town. Hollowed-out buildings, bricks, and broken windows were everywhere. Not a soul was in sight.

The building seemed deserted, but the elevator worked. Again, Wendy tried to memorize the faces of her kidnappers, but conflicting sensations distracted her. *Don't bother looking at the Fat Man and his assistant. Everyone remembers them coming into the restaurant. I remember that Joe, the delivery man, is skinny. He has sandy-brown hair and squinting eyes. The driver is muscular and looks unremarkable. Yes, his nose is slightly turned up — I'll remember that.*

By paying careful attention, Wendy estimated that they stopped on the fifth floor. There the men dumped them. The Fat Man gave them several more jabs with his feet, saying: "You'll have plenty of privacy here to fool around. Have fun with all the rats and the roaches!" He laughed sadistically again.

The door slammed shut. Wendy and David listened to the elevator whine to the ground floor. They heard the car doors shut and the engine roar off. What followed was the worst sound of all — complete silence.

~Chapter 13~

SOON AFTER THE men left, the dampness seeped through Wendy's clothes on her stomach and chest. She could hear the rain dripping into the building and see puddles of water on the ground. She thought she saw rats with beady, sinister eyes scurrying past. She had heard of rats biting children in the slums. The thought made her want to scream, but her mouth was taped shut. Her head was like a bomb about to explode. Her hands and feet were tightly bound behind her, and she felt like a sitting duck waiting for the rodents to strike. She had never dreamed that such a hideous thing could happen to her. *Oh, what can I do? What can I possibly do?*

She tried to roll onto her side, but then she heard David make stifled sounds, "Uh, uh, uh." His face had turned beet red; his eyes were bulging, and he was arching and rolling himself back and forth like a rocking horse.

Wendy did not know what he wanted. She tried to rock herself and move around too. Lunge, pull, rock — lunge, pull, rock. It was hard work. Perhaps this would keep them warm, or at least keep the rats away, she thought.

David shook his head urgently and made more of the same sounds. Wendy stopped rocking and watched him.

David nodded his head and said, "Uh, uh . . ." and rolled onto his side. Wendy did the same. David nodded his head again, went back onto his chest, and started rocking again. David continued to nod his head. Finally Wendy understood: He wanted her to lie still.

Soon he was behind her, and Wendy could feel his head touching her feet, and then her hands.

As David went on making "uh-uh" noises, Wendy felt his wet face and then the tape.

"Uh, uh, uh . . ." David rubbed his taped mouth on her fingers repeatedly. Finally, her nails lifted off a corner of the tape. Slowly, she caught hold of one end, and David pulled himself away.

"Ah." David took a deep breath through his mouth and said, "Your nails must have left cat whisker marks all over my face." He wiggled his nose and his mouth. "Ouch! That tape must have pulled out some of my five-o'clock shadow!"

Wendy tried to say, "I'm sorry! This must hurt," but only strange mumbling sounds came through the tape.

"Thank God you have nails. Now, I'll try to chew off the rope around your wrist." He proceeded to do so, spitting and losing his temper in the process. "Did you know about this kidnapping? Is this why you followed me?"

"Uh, uh, uh . . ." was all Wendy could say in response.

After a while, David had to give up chewing.

"Oh, this is impossible." He sounded exasperated. "You are not a lion, and I am not a mouse," he said, referring to Aesop's fable.

Wendy wanted to say, "I saw some rats. City rats only chew flesh, not ropes!" She was still taped up, so she went "Uh, uh, uh" and nodded to indicate that David should stay still. She began to lunge, pull, and rock again. It felt good to be active for a change. She soon positioned herself behind David and rubbed her face against his fingers the way he had done. David had more difficulty: His nails were short, and his thick blunt fingers could not grab the tape.

"Let me try to pull it with my teeth," suggested David. He started rocking and lunging again to get himself into position.

"When the Fat Man puffed smoke on me, I kept spitting out my saliva instead of swallowing," David panted. "And then I kept calling your name, 'Way Way Wong, Wendy Wong Wai Weh.' I'm sure that loosened the tape, and it became easier to pull off."

That should be easy for me, Wendy thought. *Why didn't I think of it before? After all, Grandpa had often said, "We are who we are. We must not renounce our heritage."* Her heritage included the support of her whole family, all properly named according to the family poem, which lent distinction to each generation.

Quickly, Wendy fixed a vision of her ancestors parading through her mind. Closing her eyes, she placed them in line like so many pictorial, calligraphic characters in the family poem. The ancient figures in flowing silks and benign smiles slowed her heart. Then she began reciting the names of her ancestral spirits, calling for their help and vigorously moving her mouth to achieve the right effect. Finally, she arrived at all her cousins' names: "Wong Wai Ming, Wong Wai Chin, Wong Wai Ling, Wong Wai Ying, Wong Wai Kuo, Wong Wai Weh [she included Winston and herself for good measure], Wong Wai Wah, Wong Wai Whoa . . ." The tape wrinkled around her mouth.

David finally faced her. He lunged forward, turning his head slightly to avoid stabbing his nose into her face, and tried to catch a corner of the tape with his teeth.

"Uh, um, uh, um . . ." David was too close to her and too involved with his exertions to see Wendy blush. The feel of his rough chin on her face sent a tingle scurrying over her entire body. It was so powerful that Wendy forgot how uncomfortable she was. Gathering all her reserves of self-discipline, she stayed still, allowing David to do his work.

Finally, David bit on a wrinkle of the tape and pulled it off her mouth.

"Thanks! Now, I can talk! I wish I had thought of spitting while I was gagging in the car. Let me try to chew off your rope." Wendy did not explain her recitation of her ancestors' names. She rocked herself into place and started chewing on the rope.

"How did your family find out I might be kidnapped?" David asked.

The knots were expertly tied. Wendy worked up a sweat but failed to chew off any rope.

"This chewing is not getting us anywhere. Maybe we could try lying back to back and using our fingers," Wendy suggested hoarsely.

"Okay," David puffed. "Let's give it a try."

Lunge, pull, rock — lunge, pull, rock. They tried to get aligned.

"The window of my room opens onto the alley of the restaurant. Shortly after we moved uptown, I overheard those guys selling drugs and saying that they may be getting a contract to knock off some foreign politician."

Wendy collected her thoughts and told David all the things she had overheard while practicing. "I think the two I heard outside my window were the driver and the assistant. I'm sure their voices fit those two guys in the car."

"Yeah, you have an awesome ear. You can identify them for sure."

"Last week, I heard their plan. The driver was not in the gang. He was hired to rent the limousine. The voice — I think of the assistant — said, 'The boss checked out the place yesterday.' Remember how the Fat Man and his assistant barged into our restaurant when we were working?"

"Incredible! Did you tell your family?"

"Yes . . . but . . ." Wendy didn't know what to say. She could not tell David that her family considered all Caucasians foreign devils.

"This really blows my mind! Didn't your father call the police?"

"No, they weren't sure it was serious enough." Wendy swallowed. David probably already knew that the family did not trust outsiders. She could tell him everything. "They wanted to do something by themselves to protect the Ben Zvis and, at the same time, they didn't want to scare off customers."

"So they thought they could do this on their own? Did you tell Debbie?"

"No," Wendy answered miserably. "They were afraid she might call the TV station about it."

"And they sent you to tail me?" David asked, his rising voice shaking with passion.

"Yes, to make sure nothing happened to you," Wendy replied. "At least that was the plan."

"And I thought I was so smart!" cried David. "Look where my suspicions got us. Now we're both cooked."

"Oh, David, we will get loose eventually, or someone will find us. But Ambassador Ben Zvi will surely be poisoned and the House of Wong will be shut down forever!" Her voice trailed off to a whisper, and she started to whimper.

"Please calm down, Wendy. Was Winston following you today?"

"No," Wendy said miserably. "He was watching TV, and I gave him the slip. He is really a clever kid. So eager to help! It's all my fault. I thought I could do it all by myself, and I didn't trust him to help."

"He probably would have become just another victim," David panted hopelessly.

"Oh, David, you're going too fast. We're moving in circles!" Wendy cried.

She wished she could wipe the sweat off of her forehead. Their exertions had left them both with red, shiny faces.

"Stay still and I'll come around. Listen, does anyone else know about this besides you and your family?" David was rocking very fast.

"Yes. Mr. Lee of Leaky Boots. My family always considered him one of us because he is from the same village, and he is so experienced in the business world."

By lunging, pulling, and rocking, they were finally aligned. "Can you reach my ropes?" David asked.

"No." Wendy began to sniffle and weep loudly. "I can barely touch your ropes! I can't get my fingers to the knot. Oh, what are we going to do? Who will save us now?"

Dejected and wretchedly uncomfortable, Wendy was ready to give up, when she remembered Leaky Boots.

"Talking of leaky boots, I've got an idea! Are you wearing your hiking boots now?"

"Yes." David squirmed. "I wore them today because of the rain. They don't leak."

"Let me try to reach the laces!" Wendy made a desperate lunge toward David's boots.

"Great idea!" David brightened. "If you can loosen the laces, I might be able to wiggle my feet out. The boots are a bit big, and I'm wearing thin socks." He swung his sack of arms and legs toward Wendy's hands.

"Here, here . . . I think I can reach the laces . . . Yes, I've got the butterfly knot." Wendy thought her fingers would fall off from reaching overmuch. After a good deal of contortion, the knot came loose. "Ah, this is much harder than playing the flute!" Wendy felt encouraged at this initial success.

"Here, I'll try to pull out my foot while I rock forward. You pull on my boot and rock backward." David was jubilant.

Part of the boots was caught in the tied rope, so it was difficult to take them off. After laboriously straining and pulling, they finally extracted one foot, leaving the boot still tangled in the ropes.

"Ooh wee . . . that's much worse than pulling teeth," David panted. Wendy nodded in weary agreement.

With one foot loose, David wiggled his other foot and hands feverishly while Wendy did what she could to loosen the rope.

"No, no, no. Don't pull here — higher, higher. It's a good thing the kidnappers were sloppy. They tied some rope around my boots. Now I can definitely wiggle my hands!"

After incessant tugging and wiggling, David managed to liberate one hand. Then suddenly, his hands and feet were freed. He jumped up, stretched, and cheered, "Whoopee! I thought my bones would crack under all that pressure."

"Not so loud, David! What if there are guards downstairs? Help me get loose. I can't stand this any longer!"

David kneeled down before Wendy and quickly released her. Wendy jumped up. They congratulated each other with a high five, and Wendy fell into David's arms. "Thanks, David." She began sobbing.

He held her tightly and gave her a lingering kiss. Wendy was so surprised that she had no choice but to respond naturally. A long second later, she remained stupefied. Her very first kiss! Even amid all the danger, she felt glad it was David.

"You may be a terrible spy, but you sure saved our lives with all your creative ideas!" David's voice woke her from her stillness.

"No, you saved us, with your perseverance and cool head," whispered Wendy. Her heart thumped violently. She felt like shouting, jumping, and crying in spite of her fatigue.

"It's a good thing you're called Wendy Way Way Wong. Saying your name sure helped loosen my tape!"

"It helped me loosen my tape, too." She smiled, remembering her ancestors and all her cousins with the same first two names. Had the spirits of her ancestors helped?

David finished putting on his shoes and said: "Let's go! It may not be too late to call. We've got to try to save the ambassador!"

~*Chapter* 14~

"SHHH . . . BE QUIET!" David put his finger to his mouth. "Let's make sure no one is standing guard downstairs."

They listened. They could hear the sound of steady rain, but nothing else.

"We'd better take the stairs, just in case."

The stairs were slick with rainwater and littered with debris. Wendy and David picked their way stealthily down, stopping on each floor to check for enemies. They felt like intruders and did not even dare to talk. Finally, they reached the ground floor. No one was in sight. The hired killers hadn't bothered to post any guards.

Once out on the street, David gave Wendy a little smile and whispered, "Let's go!" They ran. There were neither cars, nor stores, nor houses. The monstrous warehouses looked abandoned and desolate, just like the one they had come from. They kept on running — where to, they had no idea.

"STOP!" A young man appeared out of nowhere with a switchblade in hand, halting them dead in their tracks. The man's long, light hair fell into his eyes. His clothes were so grimy, his face so pale, and his eyes so bloodshot Wendy thought for a moment he might be another kidnap victim.

"Hand over your wallets!" The switchblade menacingly slashed the air in front of their noses.

"We . . . got kidnapped. I only have . . . some loose change," David said in short, raspy breaths, quickly emptying his pockets. "Let . . . let me keep something. I've got to call the police . . . oops!"

The youth waved his blade furiously. "Call the police? Are you crazy? Hey, Chink! Where's your cash? Hand it over, NOW!"

"I . . . I didn't bring any money," Wendy declared, stuttering. "There was no time." She also pulled out her pockets.

"How's about jewelry and watches?" The young man's blade was shaking in his hand. Was he also scared? Agitated? On drugs?

Wendy pulled off her Timex, and David parted with his class ring. The robber noticed the bruises on their wrists.

"Where you come from? How you get them scars?" shot back the mugger.

"I told you! We were kidnapped!" Wendy fumed.

"You cheat on a deal?"

"No! We've given you everything. Now, please let us go, or Ambassador Ben Zvi will be poisoned!" Wendy insisted, stamping her feet.

The young man blinked in confusion, stuttering: "I can't let you call them pol . . . lice . . ." He put his knife in his boot, keeping his eye on David. "What's this about? Blackmail? Maybe —"

He did not have time to finish. David rushed forward and gave the young thief a vigorous shove. "Outta my way!" he shouted. He pulled Wendy with him. "Run, Wendy, run!"

They did not have to worry about the pallid youth chasing after them. He was leaning into a crumbling brick wall trying to steady himself, obviously too weak to respond. For a moment Wendy pitied the mugger and thought of the drug dealers she had overheard in the alley. *They are as good as murderers,* she thought to herself. *They should meet this sorry addict.*

Those bloodshot eyes! There is no life in them! Drugs had devastated his youth, his vigor, and whatever dignity he had once possessed. The House of Wong would do well to catch those slimy dealers in the alley!

Finally they saw a car coming. "Don't . . . try to flag it down," David gasped. "We don't want . . . to be picked up by any . . . strange characters . . . in this neighborhood." They kept running.

Urged on by the danger of a poisoned ambassador and the fall of the House of Wong, they ignored the rain and the slick streets with their treacherous potholes. Both stumbled in turn and then helped each other up. There was no time to worry about sprained ankles. They sprinted on and on. They felt strangely exhilarated to use their limbs after their enforced captivity.

They spied a telephone booth on a squalid main street.

"Let's try calling from there. I think you can call emergency without money."

When they reached the old phone booth, they found it utterly vandalized. Cigarette butts, paper, crack vials, glass, and matches were strewn everywhere, and there was graffiti on every square inch. The phone line was torn off and dangling.

"I guess the city took out the phone. Everyone uses cell phones now. Too bad I didn't bring mine," David said.

"I didn't either. Oh, my God!" Wendy exclaimed. "What are we to do?"

"Let's go!" David pulled Wendy away. The two of them raced toward a stand of tenement buildings, bursting into the first store they came upon.

"Please . . . you've got to call the police!" David was out of breath.

Two seedy characters loitering in the store slipped out as soon as they heard the word "police."

"Somebody's trying to poison the Israeli ambassador!" Wendy gasped.

The old Hispanic man behind the counter did not move. He cupped one hand behind his ear. "What? What you say?"

A subway train rumbled overhead, rattling the grimy glass counter and the smudgy display cases. Everything in the store was dusty and shabby.

Huffing and puffing, Wendy went on pleading, "Please, we've been kid . . . kidnapped! . . . The police must save . . . the ambassador!"

"What? You keednappers?" The stunned old man leaned forward to hear better, his hand still cupped behind one ear. "No fooling around wif me, you hooleegans! I get cops here fars, fars!" His one hand chopped on the other.

"Please do so," David said. He was ready to admit to anything. "Please call the police."

"What treecks you keeds up to? I call police!" He finally picked up the phone and dialed in what seemed to be slow motion.

"Hello, hello! Thees ees Carlos. La Paloma bodega. I have two keeds here. They keednappers, and they wan maybe keednap somebody."

"No, that isn't true!" blurted out Wendy between bursts of panting. "We have been kidnapped. We are not kidnappers!"

"Please, keeds, be quiet. How can I talk the police when you jabbering?"

"Please let me talk to the police," David pleaded.

"Their names? What your name, son?"

"David DiVario." He thought he announced his name loud enough for the police to hear.

"And my name is Wendy — Wai Weh Wong."

"What? You wan me to way a minute?" Carlos removed the receiver and cupped his ear again. Another train roared by. "You trying to fool me?"

David snatched the phone away from the old man and hurriedly told the police their names. "Please call Ambassador Ben Zvi right away, and tell him not to eat the takeout order sent from the House of Wong. It's been poisoned!" There was a pause. Then David replied, "What? You already found out? The ambassador is okay?" David covered the phone and beamed at Wendy. "He's safe! They found out all about it! They all came through!" A voice crackled in the receiver.

"Us? Totally cool!" David grinned. "Miss Wong, they want to know if we've been hurt. Are you all right?"

"I feel great!" Wendy was too excited to acknowledge any pain.

"Really, we're both okay. We're both fine." David spoke rapidly into the phone. "Where are we? Oh, let me ask. Sir, what street is this?"

"What?" Carlos leaned forward again, straining to hear.

"Where — are — you — located?" David pronounced each word distinctly.

"I am in my store," Carlos answered with righteous indignation, standing up tall.

"I mean, what is the address of your store?" Again, David spoke slowly and deliberately. He was smiling now.

"No fresh wif me," said the old storeowner. "Eef you know to come my store, you know where you are."

"Sir, we got lost." Wendy was laughing. She recalled the days when her family's restaurant had been a hive of noise and construction. She began gesticulating and shouting, "Please tell us where we are!"

"La Paloma ees the only good bodega on this street. We haf everything."

"Great," Wendy shouted. "What is the address?"

"Thees ees near Grand Avenue in the South Bronx."

With a sense of relief, David repeated this information to the police. "Oh. You know the place? Great, we'll see you soon!" After he had hung up the phone, he mused, "I wonder how they knew we'd been kidnapped. Your father called the police to report us missing, and someone called Mrs. Ben Zvi. Mr. Lee also called the police. They've all been looking for us and are on their way here!"

"David — we did it!" Wendy started crying and laughing. She didn't know what to think.

"The police coming for you? They wan you for keednapping?" Carlos scratched his shiny baldhead, frowning. "You two stay right here, and don run away!" He ran to the door and locked it.

David hugged Wendy, laughing. "Mr. Carlos, you saved our lives. You might even receive a reward for this!"

"Really?" He pricked up his ears and his face brightened. "How moch?"

"I don't know . . . but my dad will treat you to a Chinese banquet for sure! And Dave's mom will cook you the best lasagna in town." Wendy felt free to express herself again, now that she was warm and protected in David's arms.

"Oh, I love moo goo gai pan," said Carlos. "Your dad in beesiness around here?"

But before Wendy could answer, the police arrived.

~*Chapter* 15~

"WHERE ARE YOU taking us!" David shrieked when he realized they were heading toward Harlem.

"You're the real police, aren't you?" Wendy gave David a wild look of uncertainty, though the siren, the police car, and the uniformed officer looked genuine enough. By this time, anything seemed possible.

"Sure thing!" The policeman turned around, laughing. "I'm Sergeant Romano. I'm taking you to the station house, where your parents are waiting." He pulled out his badge and let them inspect it. "What happened? Were you kidnapped?"

"Yes, but we're all right now." Wendy was quick to answer. She did not want to have to explain why they were kidnapped.

"Should I take you to an emergency room to get you checked out first?"

"No, Officer, that won't be necessary. We'd rather see our parents," David said.

"In our experience, everyone needs medical care, or at least a good cleanup, after such an ordeal. We've asked your parents to bring you some fresh clothing."

"Oh." Wendy sank into the back seat. All of a sudden she was feeling limp as a rag doll.

"Thanks," David said as he looked over at Wendy. "I think we're still a little on edge."

"No wonder!" Sergeant Romano was smiling. "That must've been some ordeal you kids went through. Are you sure you aren't hurt?"

"No, we're fine. I don't think either of us wants to face the emergency room of a hospital just now. Wendy, are you sure you're okay?" David turned to Wendy, reaching for her hand.

"Yes, I'm fine." Wendy's whole body suddenly felt renewed strength. She sat up straight. "I think I could use a shower, though." She blushed.

"You can wash up in the station house. We have a shower and some first aid kits at the precinct."

"That's okay. We're cool now." David spoke calmly and squeezed Wendy's hand. "Way Way, you look super." He was staring and smiling at her.

"You can tell us everything that happened when we get to the station house."

When they arrived, David's and Wendy's parents, along with Winston, greeted them with tearful hugs. Everyone started questioning them at once: "What happened?" "Are you hurt?" "Are you sure you're all right?" "Where did they take you?" "Did they hurt you?" "Who were the kidnappers?"

"Hold on, everybody!" Sergeant Romano held up his arm to restore order. "First we take the statements, and then you can all listen. I think the young lady would like to wash up."

"I'd like to get cleaned up, too!" David exclaimed. "We both could use a shower!" He looked at Wendy and smiled.

The Wongs and DiVarios apologized, then each mother handed a change of clothing to Wendy and David.

While Wendy was cleaning up, she went over the whole experience in her head, trying to recall every detail. She remembered being scared out of her wits. She was shivering again thinking of the acute pain she suffered at being bound and taped, the cruel fat man with the mustache menacing them with his switchblade, the cigar smoke choking her in the car, the dilapidated warehouse, the beady-eyed rats watching them try to wriggle free, and the pale young ruffian brandishing his knife. She'd prefer to forget all about it. One thing she knew for sure: In dealing with the police, she would leave the family's intrigue to her parents to explain. She would also leave out the part about Leaky Boots and the help she received from reciting the names of all her ancestors and cousins. She would start her story from the time she left the house to follow David.

When Wendy emerged from the bathroom, she found that both sets of parents had set up a feast on the station house desk. There were cartons of Chinese takeout, several pizzas, and salads. Winston was sitting in front of a plateful of lasagna. David was freshly changed and already eating and recounting to the police what had happened. Wendy joined him. No one asked her about the family's plan to save the Ben Zvis. She assumed her parents had already given their statements.

"His name is Joe," David was saying. "We heard the Fat Man call him that when he gave him instructions."

"The Fat Man was the same guy that came barging into our restaurant last week!" Wendy was quick to add.

"Now give us a description of each of these people," said one of the police officers. "How many individuals were involved?"

Wendy and David answered each question carefully. Between bites of food, they helped one another fill in the missing details. David mentioned that Joe had a missing tooth on his left side, and Wendy now remembered the Fat Man was wearing a gold diamond ring on the pinkie of his right hand.

"Mrs. Ben Zvi called earlier and asked to see you," said Sergeant Romano after the questions were over. "Are you too tired to go?" He looked at the two gleaming faces.

"Sure, we'll go," David answered. Wendy nodded and took another gulp of Orange Tang, happy that her parents had remembered to bring it. She felt strangely invigorated after the familiar food and drink.

"We had better come along too," Mr. Wong said. "We really owe the Ben Zvis an apology."

The police took the Wong and DiVario families to the Ben Zvis' apartment. They were greeted warmly by Mrs. Ben Zvi. Amid a jumble of questions and exclamations about their capture and escape, everyone examined the bruises on David's and Wendy's wrists and ankles.

Mrs. Ben Zvi took Wendy's hand, gently rubbing the chaffed areas of her wrists and arms. "I am so glad you are safe. I want to find out what happened and to thank you personally for saving my life."

"I don't know, really know, what happened," David said.

Wendy hastened to interrupt. "David saved my life because he kept calm under pressure and he was the first to work himself loose." Wendy had so much to tell, she hardly knew where to begin.

"Wendy was a great help." David was just going to tell about Wendy's fortitude, when Wendy jumped in.

"I was a wreck and I thought I had failed you terribly. Dad, what happened? Where is the ambassador?"

"The truth is," Mrs. Ben Zvi said with a smile, her light blue eyes sparkling. "The ambassador is in Israel for a secret meeting. So your alert actions saved MY life."

"Wai Weh, we told you the family was behind you one hundred percent! So you may be sure you were not left to oversee the delivery alone," Mr. Wong answered. "After our family meeting, Mr. Lee went to the ambassador's apartment building and gave the doorman a handsome tip. He instructed the doorman to call Lee Kee Boots each time David brought House of Wong food into the building. If a stranger brought the food, he was to call immediately, because he wanted to know how many delivery boys I employed. He pretended he was my competitor, and was seeking information regarding the volume of my takeout business." Mr. Wong took out his handkerchief from his pocket and wiped his face. "To be safe, Mr. Lee also called the doorman every time the Ben Zvis placed an order. He pretended he was just checking. The doorman, of course, knew David from his past deliveries. But when the assassin, and not David, showed up with the poisoned food, the doorman got suspicious and called Mr. Lee." Mr. Wong stood up, slipping his handkerchief back into his pocket. Now pacing back and forth to control his excitement, he continued. "Mr. Lee instructed the doorman to call the police and alert Mrs. Ben Zvi immediately about the tainted food. We also contacted Mrs. Horton and asked her to call Mrs. Ben Zvi to confirm the doorman's story."

Mr. Wong stood still, positioning an imaginary baseball bat over his right shoulder, and went on with his account. "The doorman was instructed to detain the delivery man. He waited quietly for the assassin, standing near the elevator with his nightstick. When the luckless fellow came down, he received a right-field hit on his head." Mr. Wong swung his bat with all his might and Winston cheered as if his father had just hit a home run. "The fellow got locked up in the elevator until the police arrived."

Wendy grinned in amazement and relief.

"I told them you had been kidnapped!" Winston interrupted, impatient to add his voice. "Grandma sent me out to catch you and bring you an umbrella, Wendy. I ran as fast as I could but couldn't find you." He walked up to his father and stood beside him like a sentry. "I waited outside the ambassador's building, and this weird guy came in with our food. I knew you must have been kidnapped, so I introduced myself to the doorman, helped him call Mrs. Ben Zvi, and ran home like lightning."

"Winston not know what happened really," Mrs. Wong explained, motioning her son to sit by her. "But Winston said you missing, so we also called police. We too worried to call Mrs. Ben Zvi ourselves, so we explained everything Mrs. Horton and asked her call Mrs. Ben Zvi. We also called Mr. and Mrs. DiVario." Mrs. Wong fidgeted with Winston's shirt collar, adding: "In fact, we so very sorry to the DiVarios, because we put David in dangerous position." Her face flushing, she could not look at the DiVarios.

"Oh, don't worry, Mrs. Wong," David answered brightly. "This was the most exciting thing that ever happened to me!"

"But we did not expect kidnapping." Wendy's mother swallowed. "Wendy heard whispers when she was practicing. How can we believe is true? We did not foresee consequences. We also called Mr. Lee every time David go to the Ben Zvis. So we thought he was protected."

"And you also asked Wendy and Winston to follow me, so they were in the same danger as I was." David added.

"Look, Mr. Wong," Mr. DiVario said. He extended an arm toward the restaurant owner. "We shouldn't get alarmed at every bizarre event that goes on in this city. Next time something strange happens in the neighborhood, come talk to me. We store owners need to look after one another."

"You can trust me too," Mrs. Ben Zvi asserted, placing a hand over her heart. "Believe me, our lives have been threatened many, many times. If you had revealed your suspicions to us, I would have sent some of our bodyguards to protect your restaurant and fetch my food."

"Ah, you are all correct." Mr. Wong sighed. He wiped his face again to hide his embarrassment. "After all your help with that Red Tag — Stop Work Order — we wanted to do something on our own to make sure no one was harmed." He paused and looked at the solemn faces of his good friends. "In truth, after so many years in America, we still do not feel completely at home. Even after we beat the Red Tag, we could not forget the stone thrown at our window. We still feel we can trust only ourselves."

Wendy was touched to hear her father confess his misgivings before so many people. "But the police saved little Eddy," she cried.

"Yes, yes, and none of you are Chinese!"

"We're all Americans!" Mr. DiVario chimed in. "Well, in spirit anyway." He nodded at Mrs. Ben Zvi.

"Dad." Winston jumped up to face his father. "You can take us all on a vacation this summer. We will see America and meet other Americans."

"Winston!" his mother reprimanded him with a stony glance, "so many good Americans here! We lucky! We get to know DiVarios and Mrs. Horton better, for sure." Mrs. Wong was not ready to leave the restaurant, not even for a vacation.

Wendy felt her face and mouth lifting up of their own accord. She was so happy at the turn of events that might lead to the fulfillment of her secret wish. Oh, it would be heaven if her family were really a part of the community and David her special friend forever! She could also tell Debbie everything after having acted so boldly. Number-One Girlfriend would approve. Her family could not possibly object now.

"Well, anyhow, I am grateful for your thorough planning to ensure my safety." Mrs. Ben Zvi smiled, nodding. "You did as good a job as the secret police!"

"Strong family builds strong character, as I always say." Mrs. DiVario noted with a smile. "I am proud of my David, and of Wendy too. They have been a pair of very brave children."

David and Wendy looked at each other and blushed.

"Are you the young lady with the attentive ear?" Mrs. Ben Zvi looked fondly at Wendy. "Was it you who overheard the assassins planning the murder?"

"Yes," Wendy whispered. "I am used to playing in the orchestra and listening out for all the other parts."

"Didn't I hear you playing 'Sunrise, Sunset' from *Fiddler on the Roof*?" Mrs. Ben Zvi grinned with amusement. "I think I heard you from the garden room."

"Yes," answered Wendy. "I'm practicing for the spring concert in school."

"Do you know that is one of my favorite tunes? Do you know who always plays it for me when he comes to visit?"

"No," answered Wendy.

"My dear friend Itzhak Perlman! Would you like to accompany Itzhak next time? I am certain he would be happy to play the overture from *Fiddler* with you."

"Oh, would I ever!" Wendy exclaimed, her eyes flashing with excitement. "Wow, I'd better go home and practice."

"Now, what would your handsome young friend want for a reward?" Mrs. Ben Zvi walked toward David, beaming up into his face.

"Oh, nothing really . . . Thanks, Mrs. Ben Zvi." David blushed. He paused and scratched his head. "Actually, there is one thing: I'd like to come and hear Wendy when she plays with Mr. Perlman."

Wendy smiled and looked very intently into David's eyes. By now no one seemed surprised at this turn of events.

On their way home Winston asked, "How did the bad guys carry you into the warehouse when you were bound up?"

"Oh, we were all trussed up, and they dragged us by the shoulders. You know, like they drag an animal to be roasted in a bonfire after a big-game hunt." Wendy grimaced.

Winston's eyes widened and glowed when he heard his sister's description. He cried: "Dad, please, please, let's take a vacation like the Americans! Let's go on an African safari!"

Wendy suddenly found herself laughing and crying at the same time. Her arms and legs ached, but her heart overflowed with joy. She hugged Winston and would not let go. She was so very, very happy to be home! She was very glad, too, "to be born Chilese, born beeg family, VELLY, VELLY GOOD LUCK!"

~READING GROUP GUIDE FOR INTRIGUE IN THE HOUSE OF WONG~

The story begins after the House of Wong restaurant moves from Chinatown to the posh Upper East Side of Manhattan. Wendy Wong keeps in touch with her best friend, Debbie, through e-mail and we learn the different cultural and physical settings of the two locations. Uptown, while the Wong family lives upstairs, the restaurant undergoes renovation. They find drug dealing occurring in the adjacent alley and vandals throw a stone at their window. Adding to the tension, the restaurant receives a "stop work order." The family is used to the clannish, insular ways of Chinatown. Their only adviser uptown is Mr. Lee, the long-time owner of the exclusive boutique Lee Kee Boots.

Fourteen-year-old Wendy and her nine-year-old brother, Winston, secretly wish for the integration of the family into their new community. Wendy is caught between her new wish and her strong ties to her traditional family. Soon, Wendy's flute playing leads her to a new friend and ally in Mrs. Horton, who owns the bookstore next door. Mrs. Horton brings the retired judge Harry Bernstein and the Israeli ambassador Ira Ben Zvi to start a legal defense fund to assist the Wongs. The family agrees to hire neighborhood help and redesign the restaurant to meet the community board's demands.

David DiVario, a senior from Wendy's high school, is hired as a delivery and bus boy. Wendy and David start a budding romance, and they learn that Ambassador Ben Zvi is a Holocaust survivor. Wendy practices the flute in her bedroom and hears voices rising from the alley under her window. The family devises a plan to have Mr. Lee call the police whenever Wendy hears drug dealing in the alley. The family is not successful in catching drug dealers. Later on, Wendy overhears a plot to poison the Israeli ambassador. The Wongs proceed to take precautions in the restaurant, but refuse to involve the police or their neighbors because they do not want to offend anyone. They trust only "people of their own kind." Wendy is instructed to tail David whenever he makes deliveries to the Ben Zvis.

At the climax of the story, David and Wendy are kidnapped by the would-be assassins, bound and gagged, and dumped in a desolate warehouse in the Bronx. However, their ingenious maneuvers and mutual cooperation help them escape. After they are freed, they find out that the family's plan has indeed saved the ambassador's life.

~QUESTIONS FOR DISCUSSION~

1. In the Chinese family, a child's duty is "to listen and obey." Do you think this is right? How do you feel about listening to and obeying adults?

2. How does Wendy balance the hopes and expectations of her family against what she wants?

3. Did the Wong family's emphasis on "harmony and cohesion" help Wendy in her efforts to integrate the family into the neighborhood, or did it hinder her?

4. The friendship between Debbie and Wendy lasted through the many changes occurring in their lives. How come? Do you think this friendship will continue when the girls mature?

5. Wendy never stood up to her family. Is she a wimp? What is she afraid of?

6. Do you think Wendy's attraction to David is physical? Was she using her family's values when she evaluated him?

7. Do you feel David is a suitable love interest for Wendy?

8. Do you find the Wong family obnoxious? Do you think they are loving? Do the children care about the family?

9. Why did Mrs. Horton want to help the Wongs?

10. Is Wendy a go-getter because she is an honor student, an accomplished flutist, and a competition winner?

11. Does the family poem make sense? What does it try to say?

12. Do you think that deep down Wendy believes in getting help from her ancestors?

13. Why do you think David finds Wendy attractive?

~ABOUT THE AUTHOR~

 **Amy S. Kwei** is a graduate of St. John's University (BA) and Vassar College (MA). She retired from teaching psychology in New York at Bennett College and Dutchess Community College. She has twice won the Talespinner Competition, sponsored by the *Poughkeepsie Journal.* One of the judges, Michael Korda, wrote: "*[The Visit]* has a very strong cultural appeal, and gives the reader a quick, instant understanding of Chinese values, and how they differ from our own. As well, it is simply written, perhaps the best written of all the stories here."

Her short stories and essays have appeared in *Prima Materia, Short Story International, CAAC Inflight Magazine, Westchester Family, Dutchess Magazine, The Country,* and *Dutchess Mature Life.* Andover Green published one of her children's stories in *Six Inches to England, An Anthology of International Children's Stories.*